AN ANGEL

WITH

SILVER WINGS

JAMES KEIR BAUGHMAN

CONTENTS

DEDICATION

IT APPEARED on the front page of Fort Walton's weekly Playground News, Thursday, July 28, 1949. The article was painfully brief in contrast to the shock and stunned sadness we felt on Eglin Air Force Base's Auxiliary Field #1 at dawn's roll call Wednesday morning.

BULLETIN

First Lieutenant Roy H. Amidon, Jr. was killed Tuesday night during a routine training mission from an auxiliary field at Eglin Air Force Base. He was a member of the 117th Fighter Group, Alabama Air National Guard.

The cause of the crash is not known immediately. A board of Air Force officers has been appointed to investigate. Amidon is survived by his wife Geraldine S. Amidon, 1509 44th Street, Bellview Heights, Birmingham Alabama and his father A.H. Amidon of Lakeland Florida.

The July 28th edition of the unit's hometown newspaper, the Birmingham News, with a photo showing him to be a fine looking young man, offered a bit more.

Amidon, in fact a Second Lieutenant, had been in Birmingham for only two or three years and a pilot in the Air Guard unit for just nine months. He was the first local Air Guard pilot to die in a crash since the unit had been formed after World War II.

The article explained that his P-51 fighter crashed as it came in for a landing, that he was 24 years old, had served as a fighter pilot in the Air Corps during World War II..., and that he was part owner of Central Park Garage at 1416 Bessemer Road.

Also made clear was that funeral services would be held in Lakeland, Florida.

More of his life was shared in Wednesday evenings July 27th edition of the Lakeland Ledger.

Roy was, in fact, a Floridian, born and reared in Lakeland, graduated from Lakeland High School, where he and his soon-to-be-wife Geraldine played in the school band. He was the son of prominent Polk County Criminal Judge Roy H. Amidon, Sr and Mrs. Amidon, as the paper termed it in those more formal years. His age, better defined now, was actually 25.

Members of the 160th Fighter Squadron of the Alabama Air National Guard..., to which Lt. Roy Amidon's 117th Fighter Group was attached...were to fly in formation over the grave at Oak Hill Cemetery during interment.

His parents and his grandfather L.E. Amidon had been summoned home from a vacation in New Hampshire because of the tragedy. Sadly, they had intended to stop by in Birmingham to visit Roy and Geraldine the following Sunday during their planned trip home at the end of their vacation.

Dedication

A few sentences of the article point out the confusion which often surrounds such a sudden calamity.

"It was assumed..." the article said, "...that Lt. Amidon's wife had been notified by the National Guard of the death and had in turn called Judge Amidon in New Hampshire."

That's the one facet of Roy Amidon's story this writer knows. When we drew to attention at roll call that dawn, our unit leader was missing. He was a best friend of Roy and Geraldine. Immediately, in late night hours, he left Eglin's Auxiliary Field #1 to make the five hour drive home... to tell her personally of Roy's passing.

Our ache was not only for Lt. Roy Amidon's crash and death...but for her shock and sorrow..., and the painful moments our friend and unit boss would face in the breaking of terrible news.

There is nothing of the Angel, of this curious story, that speaks of Roy Amidon's experiences in life. 17 year old privates never...never... hobnob with officers. This writer never met Roy, knew nothing of him until that awful morning. In truth, we found only after his passing that our unit leader was his best friend. Details of his life were discovered only in recent days, through research in three now aged newspaper articles... long after this story was written.

I wonder why the sense of shock and sorrow of that morning has lingered for more than a half century? Is that what separates one who yearns to write from those not so inclined?

It is surely true that the anguish of that long ago morning..., awe of the magnificent P-51...,

Dedication

and maybe the hope of Angels ..., were the well-spring from which this strange tale flourished.

You may see now, though, why this story is dedicated not only to the memory of Second Lt. Roy H. Amidon, Jr..., to past and present fellow members of his Alabama Air National Guard at Birmingham...but to all of America's brave citizens who give of their time, and face the risks, of serving as Guardsmen and Reservists...vital, immediate back up to Armed Regulars..., America's massed second line of defense.

ACKNOWLEDGEMENT

As we blossom forth into more mature years, ponder our span of time, we'll more than likely find a deeper sense of understanding for the manner in which others have influenced our lives. Truth is, every being with whom we interact contributes..., whether in the most complimentary of ways...or in sore conflict.

Those closest, greatly admired, essential in daily endeavors, become a power in our growth, truly helping to mold our personalities, making us what we are. In a very real sense each becomes a part of our being.

If you doubt...think over the many things you say, do, believe, feel...and then remember who first shared the vision with you. The roster will not be brief, longer as years gather. Remembrances of certain ones radiate, as fireflies on a dark night.

It was a Monday in 1959, barely an hour before midnight, that I first met such a friend.

Mondays were long then at Fort Walton Beach's weekly Playground News...now our Northwest Florida Daily News. That one day of the week stretched from 8:00 or so in the morning to 2:00 or 3:00 o'clock, far into wee hours of the night. The season was mild, demanding neither heat nor air conditioner...a delightful time of year with few bugs. That allowed us to leave the door wide ajar, and crank slender glass slats of jalousie windows open to let in night fragrance.

Acknowledgement

It was advertising layout I was intensely concentrating on, striving to get as many ads finished as possible before the courier came from Pensacola at 1:00 a.m. to pick up the fruits of our labor.

Far unexpected at that hour, suddenly, with hurried, long-legged stride, in through the open door came - what appeared to be - a Catholic Priest.

"Oh good grief," I muttered silently. "What now? Not another ad! I have no room for it. I'd have to lay out the whole darn paper again."

Pastor Robert L. Keys was not Catholic, but Lutheran...whatever that was, I thought in the moment. Tall, slender, with close trimmed dark hair, already balding a bit at 31, he was older than many ministerial graduates. He'd already achieved a business degree, worked a while in the corporate world, before he felt the call, and embarked on four more years of college..., seminary, of course, this time.

He introduced himself as a "mission" pastor, gathering together the first Lutheran congregation in our area. It seemed..., though I carefully didn't say it..., a bit of an insult. Ours were, admittedly, tiny towns in those years, a bit wild, military, touristy with more than our share of bars and night clubs.

But we had a plenty of churches too...Baptist Methodist, Catholic, Episcopalian, Presbyterian, the Church of Christ, Congregational. How could we possibly be classified as a "mission" area? As it turned out that's what Lutherans term all formative churches.

Acknowledgement

Mentioning that my wife happened to be Lutheran grabbed his attention. That led soon to attending some of his first services held in McLaughlin Funeral Home's Chapel. (As a matter of history, the McLaughlins, well known business and civic leaders in our Emerald Coast's developmental years, helped found several new churches in that way). Persuaded to transfer membership from lifelong Methodism, led me to service on one of Bob's first church councils, and then as an early church treasurer. It was a youthful first venture into civic service.

As it turned out, Bob Keys was from Allentown, PA, also my wife's home town. He quickly became more than Pastor... a personal friend who often visited and shared meals in our home. Tending to be softly spoken in manner, there was still quiescent determination, a gentle driving force, about his sermons and his work.

The age of 27 is deemed fully "mature," of course, though there will likely be amazing innocence yet to be discovered. I assumed, for instance, that all of a pastor's needs and concerns must be heavenly attended, wholly fulfilled.

In keen contrast, Bob Keys was unmarried, and intensely lonely, though a genial composure and gentle, witty personality covered it smoothly. Moreover, accustomed to far larger, bustling, Allentown, he acutely disliked our tiny town atmosphere. Truth was, Bob intimated regularly to his boss, our Florida Synod Bishop - with tongue-in-cheek-witticism - that he'd been delegated to a "foreign" mission.

Worse...though he seldom showed it...Bob

Acknowledgement

Keys was far from elated with twelve to fourteen hour days, seven day work weeks, the ongoing stress, the awesome uncertainty of finding, gathering together, organizing, funding, planning, molding a congregation from scratch. And atop that wondrous workload is the even more major task of funding, designing, and erecting a church building to house the new multitude. In moments of sheer stress Bob grumbled, nicely enough, that he would never do it again. He never did.

In 1961, a couple of years before our church building was finished, he left us to serve eight years as a Navy chaplain. Then afterwards, the balance of his ministerial career was tendered as a pastor in central Florida. He remained always unmarried

Upon retirement, Bob chose a condominium in Sebring, Florida and a second home in the mountains of North Carolina.

In late summer of 2003 he came to Fort Walton Beach to visit the few of us who knew him well, those of us who remain as charter members of Holy Trinity. He looked in perfect health, slimmed down, trim, just as he was when we first met him in 1959, enjoying retirement years.

Six months later, he was gone. The illness which took him came suddenly, a few weeks of spiraling worse and worse.

Oddly, when we asked our Florida Lutheran Synod leaders for more information for our records on his education, background, and long career...they seemed to know little of him. Churches, it seems to me, sometimes foment the most aberrant ways of doing things.

Acknowledgement

Here in vastly grown Fort Walton Beach, we know that Pastor Robert L. Keys left an abundant legacy in our Holy Trinity Lutheran Church, now approaching it's forty-fifth anniversary. Today, it's membership surpasses six hundred ...far more than the seventy-six Lutherans who gathered in McLaughlin Funeral Home's Chapel to sign the church Charter on October 25th 1959. In truth, though, Bob left this writer one more legacy, as he surely did for many others. Experience in Holy Trinity's busy founding, moved me to join others, and continue to work through civic and public service organizations...City Council, Regional Planning Council, Florida League of Cities, Okaloosa County Gas District, Lions Club, Civil Air patrol, YMCA, Coast Guard Auxiliary, Junior Achievement, Chamber of Commerce, Jaycees, to name a few ...striving to make our home town, as Bob Keys made our church, a better place.

Most fruitful, perhaps, was ten years spent serving to make HeadStart and our Community Action Program more meaningful to those who especially deserve a better chance to learn and grow.

And later, for a number of years, our Holy Trinity Lutheran Church provided space for HeadStart classrooms. I don't think Bob Keys ever knew...his visits were few over the many years after he left us..., but he would have been proud of that.

PROLOGUE

In times we call our second millennium, belief in an existence that continues onward beyond this life far predates the faiths that resound today on planet Earth.

From generations of scholarly research, we know that archaeologists regularly find, in shards of ancient societies, long enshrouded evidence...bowls of food, tools, personal possessions, modes of transport meant to aid a revered, or loved, one on an end-of-life passage to whatever they called eternal Heaven.

In truth, Jewish religious belief, reaching back over 5,000 of those years, not only affirms faith in that ethereal omnipotence, but inscribes more than one hundred encounters between our human throng and heavenly Angels. From where, pray tell, would Angels come, if not from a life that parallels, or endures on, from our own?

The Christian faith, it's New Testament linked steadfastly to Jewish tradition and it's Torah, (the Christian Old Testament), spans the last 2,000 of those Jewish years, ever more eloquently speaking of Angels. In fact, it records near two hundred more of such concourse between "heavenly beings" and "us," beginning even in Genesis, the very first chapter.

Millions upon millions of the faithful are sure that every word, every happening, every encounter, in those Scriptures is absolute truth...the unfailing, infallible Word of God.

Prologue

If so...the reality of Angels must surely be of that same certainty.

But then... comes our 20th Century... with it's massive eruption of scientific and technological invention, innovation, education...advancing so many of us to override faith with science. Of course, that science has brought wonderful progress for humanity. But it has also made us wonder in uncertainty of anything that cannot be "proved" by a "scientific" experiment.

Oh, many - now and then - still find miracles in our struggling lives. But in deference to the "modern" we label them "good fortune," or curious, favorable "coincidences".

And the idea of Angels becomes less sure... more yoked with mirage... unless, perhaps, on Sunday morning... in a Hymn ...or Psalm.

So...with these thoughts, in this way... we'll leave you to rejoice in this unlikeliest of Angels, to wonder if he truly appeared in such outlandish fashion ...on such a beautiful, mundane morning...in a quiet forest... for what seemed such a worldly reason ... along one of America's most beautiful sea sides.

Perhaps, more entrancing...we'll leave you with another contemplation...a tantalizing hint.

Most every writer... even in this free flowing genre called creative fiction...writes of many things that are not of fantasy... but real, true, touchable. After all, where else could descriptions, and ideas, images, hopes, dreams come from..., rather than from the writer's own experience... from the things he, or she, has seen and heard and lived.

It is so in this curious, colorful tale. But you, dear reader, are free to sort it all out, perhaps more fruitfully than the writer... to separate fact, truth...from hope and dream.

JAMES KEIR BAUGHMAN

AN ANGEL

WITH

SILVER WINGS

CHAPTER ONE

SO ASTOUNDING, SO INCREDIBLE, was the day, the happening..., it was only long after that he could wonder about it, about them, in the more profound sense. Might it be only in times of wretched uncertainty, fear, great peril that they reach out to us, physically touch our lives? Or may they be devoted comrades, always near, imploring, admonishing, subtly guiding us?

Where it happened - where it began, to be more precise - is an unlikely place, a delightful indulgence when there's no hurry, a cosmos of woodland and peace, inviting as a fireside chair. The lean torrent of asphalt, shimmered in summer heat-devils of subtropical sun, clings idly to low, rolling hills, snaking easy curves through pine and scrub-oak forests. Its route is far from the main highway. It's travelers the few who happen to know of its shorter path.

Like so many places in Northwest Florida, the Bob Sikes Road is named for one who served

1

thirty-eight years in the Congress of the United States.

DeFuniak Springs, dozing county seat of wooded, rural Walton County is at an end of it. Forty miles to the south, along the sun-drenched Emerald Coast, lie bustling seaside towns...Fort Walton Beach, Destin, Mary Esther, Niceville, Valparaiso, Navarre, Sandestin, Seaside.

He'd stopped there only now and then in the four decades, the last time a half-score years before. He wondered, as he drove, if he'd still recognize it.

A right turn from the Mossyhead Highway brought morning sun full into his face. Half blinded, he pawed upwards to tug down the car's visor, at the same time slowing, squinting, searching the scrubby woodland intently for the tell-tale arc leading off the road's right side.

There!...after a half-mile or so... where green, timid hills flatten into sandy-footed forest, across from an old, abandoned military railroad, was the sweeping curve. In an instant it seemed again like an old friend.

His being - the thought soared un-beckoned - seemed like that veering sprawl of faded asphalt disappearing into the forest, a going that seemed uncertain now, meaningless.

Still, the glimpse of the place buoyed his spirits, rushed his senses with heady remembering, as it had each time he'd come. Those two weeks, a lifetime before, had always loomed large..., a half-moon span of growing, seizing of new experience, reaching eagerly to touch raw edges of manhood.

Perhaps it was a need to think of dawning rather than sunset that drew him there that day. Most of us broach that at some point in our years. Comfortable it can be, in doubt and uncertainty, to peer backward, to luxuriate in a time that is now safe and secure, where wondering has been answered, dangers past...to think of friends ever-young, remember old dreams which have borne us out of youth, over years of life.

He knew it was there, a few more moments unseen, a few hundred feet ahead. While it was still hidden by the curving edge of the forest, he felt anticipation's tingle, an uneasiness, a wavering. Surely, the old entrance must have changed, its gate rusted away, perhaps built anew.

What astonished him when it loomed into view, was an electrifying, sense of life's fealty, steadfastness, perseverance. Far unexpected it was, to find it so much the same. Fence wire was rusty, as it had been long ago. Tinges of green

3

moss daubed soft, living color onto weather-grayed fence posts. The galvanized metal gate, dangling tiredly on slouched hinges, yawned a-wide, no longer giving a damn who invaded the small outpost.

The white board sign on the fence was chalky, faded. He had to stop the car to read it's once raven, sun-paled letters ..."Eglin Auxiliary Field #1." Warner Air Force Base was it's formal chris-tening, a name known to few others, by then.

Just beyond the gate he remembered the cluster of white wooden buildings rushed into being during frantic, early years of World War II. Now they were gone, long since rotted, demol-ished, leaving an eerie emptiness except for the towering steel hulk of a city-sized water tank.

Head tilted back, hand shading eyes from the glare of morning sun, he gazed high through the car's open window at its fat, familiar, towering mass. It stood at military attention, lone survivor of the outpost, a forgotten sentinel amid pine trees grown to maturity in years since the summer of 1949.

At speed little more than a walk, he rolled the few hundred feet to the center of the little base, near the old flight line, letting the small dark-blue sedan drift to a halt. He sat quietly for a moment or two, then opened the door, stepped out of the car to look around, straining to recapture the feel of the place as he'd known it, pulsing with life.

What came first to his senses was sheer quiet, barrenness. The only sound was wind, brushing through green pine needles half a hundred feet, and more, above his head.

Faded, deeply cracked streets and weathered concrete foundations marked the places where barracks and other buildings had stood. Fresh paint on the water tower, fire hydrants, the diminutive utility sheds told him the compound was still cared for, held in reserve for the day it might be needed again.

His eyes searched the streets and foundations, trying to piece together again the layout of the little base. Was this the spot where his barracks had been? He closed his eyes, picturing in his mind the row of double bunks in the barracks bay. Were there three rows or four? Were there six or eight of them sharing that small room?

Was that where the PX had been, where he'd fathomed the not-yet-familiar taste of barely chilled beer? And there...surely...that was the spot where the flight line operations shack vibrated to the sounds of thundering engines, props blasting at air.

It was the leg cramp he remembered, then. Deep in the night! Pain in the calf of his leg so sharp, so strong it ripped him from sleep. Forgetting he was in the top bunk, he'd rolled out of bed to stand, stretch, ease the agonized muscle. He relived the deep fall, crashing heavily to the wooden floor, landing unbalanced on his feet, pitching forward onto knees, hands, the force of his fall echoing, shuddering through the old barracks. In the light and warmth of morning, he laughed aloud, alone, at the memory of the muttered grumbles and curses of buddies roused from sleep by the din.

And, too, there had been a late afternoon, duties finished for the day, buddies seated on bunks playing poker before evening chow. He could feel again the heavy sense of fatigue. They'd been out 'til nearly dawn the night before, drinking in the saloons, cruising the tiny beach town, partying on the beach. Tossing in his poker hand he'd stretched out behind his pals on the khaki blanket, just to rest his eyes for a minute.

He awoke, groggy, surprised that sleep had drifted in unsought. As his eyes came to grips with the real world again, it was those same steel legs of the water tower that had loomed through the dusty barracks window. The sun, just above the horizon, had cast weak yellow rays through pine and scrub-oaks, stretching long, sunset shadows onto the base. There had been the first hint of milder air, eagerly welcomed at the setting of summer's sun in the deep south. He could feel again, so clearly, the sleepy confusion, the uncertainty. Was it evening...or morning? The sun hovered through tranquil, languorous minutes of earth's day when dawn and sunset are so much akin. His buddies were still hunched on the edges of their bunks. Laughs of victory, groans of loss droned on. Had they played poker all night while he slept?

It's the way young men are, boys yet in part, ever quick to grab the chance to taunt a buddy. Answers to his sleep confused question had come from poker faces, solemnly unanimous.

How long had they taunted him? Standing there in sunshine of a morning forty years later he relived long, muddled minutes before someone lifted the confusion, conceded that it was the sun's setting that hued the Florida sky, reminding that hunger would still be eased by evening chow, breakfast yet a welcome night's sleep away.

7

It felt good, peaceful, to relive it. He leaned against the car, let his mind drift back over years, searching in tiny alcoves of his senses, for the sounds, the sights, the feelings that had filled this small, transient, warrior's village near the end of the 1940's.

Hesitantly, at first, then more nimbly, images meandered back...the light tan uniforms of summer, big snarling olive-drab trucks called "six-bys," lurching groggily to attention at dawn's roll call, pungent odors from kerosene stoves, steaming water used to scrub mess kits, peeling potatoes on mess hall duty, the aberrant tastes of food cooked in ten gallon pots.

There were voices, faces long unseen, pictured in unchanging youth. Fred...tall, sapling thin, more boyish in countenance than his nineteen years. He'd always softened military curses into words near tolerable in polite company. Fred's 1946 Plymouth carried six of them, convertible top open, wind whipped, sunburned, from Alabama's largest city to backwoods Florida for summer camp.

Ralph was not quite as tall. His droll, mischievous grin and earthy humor infused fun into everything the gang did. He drank more than enough from the gallon jug of whiskey sours they'd bought at Main Street's Magnolia Club and waded, uniform and all, out into the ocean surf. Rocked by thundering waves, barely visible in night illumined by the slimmest of crescent moons, he gleefully outran his would-be rescuers. Sober enough to be truly fearful for his life in big, surging waves, his buddies raced to catch him as he ran splashing, splattering, up and down the surf line. Teaming up three-on-one they finally grabbed him, chest deep in foaming breakers, dragged him, giggling, back to sugar white shores, ...to safety.

Fred's convertible took them, unsteadily to be sure, west on highway 98, over Brooks Bridge and the narrow waters of Santa Rosa Sound, through the tiny night-silent villages of Fort Walton and Valparaiso and Niceville into the dark, piney woods of Northwest Florida. Thirty miles to the Bob Sikes Road and the barracks of Auxiliary Field #1 took a long time. Fred drove slowly, weaving unsurely, hand over one eye to compensate for whiskey's double vision.

Ralph slept the sleep of too many whiskey sours, feet thrust out of the car's open window into the night wind. At dawn's reveille, shoes that had carried him into ocean waves were neatly side-by-side under his iron bunk, caked with salt

9

and sand, leather rock hard, unwearable, toes curled sharply upward like the green slippers of an Irish elf.

Kemp, sergeant of their small radio direction-finding unit, was one of two World War veterans among them. His tale of a dark night on the South Pacific island of Leyte in 1944 held the younger guys spellbound. There was, his war story went, a sharpness pressed suddenly into the back of his neck. It was well known that Japanese snipers were skulking along perimeters of the base. He'd stiffened with fright fearing a Japanese bayonet, followed by a bang, a bullet in the head. Kemp's un-tried lads, wanting to hear the story over and again, laughed uproariously as he acted out overwhelming relief, finding he'd backed into a sharp-spined bush as he relieved himself in the dark outside his radio truck.

Only part-time soldiers, not yet familiar with the reality of sudden death in war, could find humor in the fact that a man might die because he stepped outside in the dark to take a leak.

Chapter Two

It was a sound that tore him from the past, vaulted his attention from long before to the brightness of morning. It was familiar, oddly out of place. It should have been part of the remembering, but there it was...somewhere, low, just over the trees, growing rapidly louder, headed towards him.

"A Rolls-Royce 'Merlin'." He muttered the words half aloud, eyes eagerly scanning thin patches of blue sky through pine-green. Even through the mists of decades, he was not surprised that he could instantly name the purring, throbbing, snarling engine rushing toward him, yet unseen.

Designed by the British during fearful early months of the war, it gave life to three of the most famous fighter aircraft of World War II. Britain's Supermarine Spitfire saved England during the aerial Battle of Britain in 1940. America's Lockheed P-38 'Lightning' had two of those engines. The American P-51 Mustang changed the face of aerial warfare when it entered combat in Europe.

Every plane, together with the howl and throb of it's engine, has a certain air, a familiar resounding, like a kindly voice from home. It was the moan and whine and whistle of air streaking over wing and tail and nooks and crannies of the fuselage that finally assured him, before he could see.

There!...gleaming silver, quick glimpses through the treetops, like watching a fast moving car through a picket fence. Racing into the open, a hundred feet above the trees, hurtling toward where he knew the runway must be.

Yes! Of course! It was what his ears had foretold...a P-51 Mustang, the darting airborne stallion of World War II.

Suddenly, smartly, a bank to the left, nose up, the silvery fighter surging upward in a steep, tight climbing turn, landing gear snapping outward at the top of the curve where centrifugal force is the greatest, landing flaps on the back edge of the wings coming down.

Around the tight arc of the turn, not quite upside down now, diving downward, long slender engine nacelle seeking the runway, exhaust of the engine's twelve cylinders crackling with backfire as throttle is pulled back. That sound, that singular, clattering, flamboyant backfire, like a signature flourish...is so much a part of the Mustang's character.

As it slowed, glided smoothly toward landing the plane disappeared again behind trees. The small base, unlike most, was not by then on the open field alongside runways. The site where buildings, aircraft parking areas called tarmac, and operational facilities had been located were between the ends of two intersecting runways, hidden from them by a screen of trees. Or, truth be told, it was likely the obstructing forest had grown from empty fields since the time of world War II.

He thought the plane would accelerate, roar off again in flight practice aviators call "touch and go." But he could hear it slow, stop, engine revving as it turned around, taxi back toward him.

Two hundred yards away it appeared amid pines and scrub oaks, rounding a final turn in the taxi strip, engine in loping idle. Following the blurred arc of it's huge whirling propeller, it rolled quickly, smoothly onto the tarmac and came to a stop near him. The engine slowed. With final lurch of the prop it was still.

CHAPTER THREE

QUIET AGAIN SWEPT over the barren little base as he watched the plexiglas bubble of the plane's cockpit canopy slide back. The pilot sat a few moments more, flipping switches, finishing the engine shutdown procedure.

Finally, he climbed out of the cockpit, slipped parachute straps off his shoulders. Dropping the chute on shiny, riveted metal, he hopped lithely to the ground from the backside of the wing, and walked toward him.

"Hey, how ya' doin'?," the pilot greeted, still walking, a dozen steps away. His voice was strong, a bit commanding, not quite arrogant, grin broad, out-going. His gait and posture radiated relaxed self assurance.

"Great! How about you?" It was his usual answer to a greeting, even on days when he didn't feel it.

"Can't complain," the pilot said thrusting out his hand, "I'm Rob." The handshake was firm, strong. He noticed that the pilot was four inches or so shorter than his own six foot one inch height, tanned, leanly athletic looking, an aura of energy and contained aggressiveness about him. Weren't they all like that? Colossal egos. Cut from a mold... every one. Different from ground soldiers who fought in squads, companies, regiments. Perhaps necessary in war, in the one-on-one job they were trained to do. But far too many of their wives and children and mistresses found their me-first, win-at-any-cost, whiskey-soaked, wow-'em-and-move-on, here-today-gone-tomorrow personalities left far less than joy in their wake. Likeable all - at first - exciting to many women, but over years in a military town he'd grown wary of them.

"Jemison Thorsby," he responded, making sure his own hand grip was equally firm.

"OK, pal! Thor it is! Saw you down here by yourself." The pilot reached to his face, took off gold rimmed, tear drop, aviator sunglasses. Those dark glasses, battered leather bomber jacket, floppy officer's hat, untanned circles around the eyes...were all manifest, even postured, trademarks of the World War II fighter pilot. "Something wrong with your car?"

It was the eyes that were different. So very different! Compelling! He was taken aback, hesitant in reply. It wasn't simply that the eyes were

15

such pale green, clear, penetrating, direct. There was something deeper, elusive. Unexpected warmth, personal interest, even...yes, perhaps that was it...a near glowing of inner sincerity that belied the pilot's outer offhanded manner.

"No. No problem..." His demeanor grew subtly more guarded. "The cars okay. I stopped by what's left of old Auxiliary Field #1 this morning. You know...just to reminisce a bit. I do it every now and then."

"Good enough, pal. So do I. You live around here?"

"Long time. Forty years or so."

"How 'bout that? Often wished I could live here." An odd wistfulness suffused his features. "It's different here, special somehow. Beaches are so clean and white, almost like sugar. And the sea...it's really such an unusual blue-green color. I never see many people...I mean not like a big city. Not really very much traffic. So much forest and uncrowded space."

"It's got it's faults," Thorsby nodded. "There's heat and humidity in summer. The towns are small, so there's not much shopping or entertainment. Good jobs are not that easy to find. It's sure a good place to live, though, if you like sailing or fishing, the beach, things like that."

"Fishing..." the pilot's gaze lifted, moved beyond. "My wife liked to fish. Lot of wives don't, I guess. Her dad had a cabin up on the Warrior River in Alabama. Some of our best times were there. We went whenever we could."

The pilot was oddly quiet for a moment, pensive.

"If I'd known how little time we had...." More than wistfulness now, there was fleeting sadness in his eyes.

The flyer himself severed the moment, shoved away melancholy. His smile reappeared, "Looks like we both come back to this deserted old field now and then," he said changing the subject, gesturing toward empty streets and foundations. " Why do you come back?"

"It's just that I was stationed here a long time ago. Only two weeks. But, it was...well, a good time, you know? Nice to remember now and then."

"Hey! So was I!," the pilot said. "When were you here?"

"July, 1949. It was an Alabama Air National Guard summer camp. We had unit's from seven states, the biggest Air National Guard exercise ever held up to then."

"Right, pal!," the pilot laughed. "Sounds like we were here at the same time!"

"You?...In July '49?...from Birmingham?" He glanced past the pilot's shoulder, to the plane. On the fuselage were the words "Alabama Air National Guard." That seemed odd, though, confusing.

"Yo! The old 117th Fighter Wing under the 217th Bomb Group. I worked for the telephone company during the week, flew Air National Guard on weekends."

"Same unit I was in!" He laughed, astonished, glad, delighted to meet someone from that time. "Amazing isn't it? Bumping into each other out here, in the middle of nowhere?"

"You know what they say...," the pilot's chuckle was easy, relaxed. "The Good Lord works in mysterious ways."

"Where'd you get the old P-51?...rebuild her yourself?" As he spoke, the sense of an oddity, a strangeness grew stronger, uneasy intuition that something was out of place, a nagging at the back of his consciousness.

"Ya' see, pal, where I am now everything's new again. We can keep things like that, things that mean a lot." The pilot's tone, for the first time, seemed less offhand. "What do you think of the Mustang?"

"It's...it's just a helluva plane...the top fighter in World War II...,"he hesitated, fumbling for the right words. "Seems to me, the best looking fighter ever built."

"Yeah! Me too."

"Always wondered what it's like to fly it. Does it really handle as well as they say?"

"You bet! It's a great bird to fly," the pilot said, "...if you know what you're doin'. It's fast, tricky, better than most. Every fighter, though, has a quirk that'll kill you, if you let it."

"I've heard if you let it get too low, too slow, then jam the throttle forward...the power, the big prop...it'll just roll you over into the ground!"

"True enough," the pilot nodded, "true enough!" He glanced up at pale blue of the sky. "Easy to avoid, though. Watch your airspeed, ease the throttle forward. Like ridin' a bike, it's not hard to stay up when you know how!" He brushed the fault aside with a wave of his hand. "You know, before I..." he hesitated, "...back when I was in the squadron, I often flew down here. I'd cruise around, do a few rolls, shoot some touch and go's, buzz the beaches. You know!"

19

"Sure!...Then I'll bet you put it down on the main base, got a steak, and checked out the babes at the officers club!" he rolled his eyes, his chuckle knowing, suggestive.

The pilot tarried again, suddenly awkward, some sort of discomfort obvious. "Sure. Lunch. Sometimes dinner. Every now and then, over-night in the BOQ. But the other, the girls..." He seemed to be looking for the right words. "Easy pickin' for a lot of fly-guys I guess. I just never...," his voice faltered, rummaging for the way to say it. "My wife and I went through high school, a year of college, together. She meant so much to me. We got married after flight school, just be-fore they sent me to England."

"I didn't mean..." he in turn fumbled for words, embarrassed by his assumption, misjudgment, of lumping one with many. "It's not the wives...it's the others they brag about."

"Yeah, the guys think it's sport, a game, a score! The girls are star-struck, willing, easy tar-gets for the pilots," the pilot grinned, less sure, self-conscious. "Somehow, I was just never able to think of that as a casual or passing thing." He looked away, thoughtful. "Maybe I didn't come up to 'ye olde' fighter pilot womanizing standards in that respect."

Uneasy with the words, with the explanation, the flyer seemed to need to say more. "Once, a few months after I got to England, one of the girls at the Officer's Club asked me to walk her home. She was there a lot, dated a lot of the guys. Seemed a great idea at first that night. We'd had a few drinks. I was lonely. She was pretty. You know how it goes."

"Sure."

"It wasn't far. I mentioned I was married. It didn't seem to matter much. When we got to her flat, up three flights of stairs, she invited me in."

"The plot thickens!," a wry laugh, lightening the sharing of it.

"Yeah, but by then...," the pilot looked down, studied a patch of brownish-green grass, "...all I could see was my wife's face. All I could feel was how much I ached to see her, how much I cared about her, no one else." The pilot's eyes reached again to that far distant time and place. "I couldn't get out of there fast enough," he glanced up, brightened. "Made some lame excuse, left her at the door. Trotted about ten blocks back to base. We were in pretty good physical shape then." He paused, quiet for a long moment.

"I guess I wasn't very surprised by my reaction," he finally added, smiling again. "Taught me

21

a lesson, though. I stayed away from situations like that from then on. I just concentrated on doing my job! All I really wanted was to fly, anyway. Just trying as hard as I knew how to get home in one piece."

Silence grew, stretched, lingered...born of the difficulty men, among their own, have in expressing empathy, what might be taken as wimpishness. Perhaps it's only when such values are plainly shared that men can voice them at all.

"So...you saw aerial combat?" Thorsby bridged the shared silence, moved the conversation on to more comfortable things. All the while, growing unease, a swelling apprehension nagged at the back of his mind...a towering, enveloping sense that he was missing something. Something obvious, fundamental, crucial.

"I got there late in the war," the pilot's tone was again assured, back in familiar territory. "The Luftwaffe was pretty well shot up by then, not much going on in the air. I had two kills. Nothing to feel great about. One was a real dogfight, a Focke-Wulf 190. Fine airplane, but the pilot must have been awfully young... or very poorly trained."

"If they send the wrong guy, they lose the plane, right?"

"Yeah," the pilot nodded, continuing. "The other was a cargo plane, a three engine Junkers 52. It was slow, unarmed, a sitting duck for a P-51. It was a general's plane, though. If he was aboard, it helped shorten the war. I got in most of my twenty five missions doing strafing runs... shooting up trains, trucks, tanks, things like that."

"With the invasion in France, armies moving on into Germany, those air attacks on ground targets knocked out a lot of enemy equipment and supplies. It was really important work!"

"Sure," the pilots grin was self conscious. "But when you're 24..., trained for air to air combat, one-on-one, dogfights...anything else is drudgery."

There!...That was it!...24 in the mid '40s. Add 4 or 5 years to 1949. More than 40 years to now. The numbers raced silently through his head like a tumbling mountain stream. This man had to be at least ten years older than his own 59 years. And yet...and yet...! There he stood, looking 28 or 30. Youthful, vigorous, vital.

"Would you like to see the P-51?" the pilot turned, motioned him onward, moving toward the plane.

Hesitantly he followed, lagging, uncertain now, unease surging, looking intently at the aviator.

23

The man should be near 70. Why was there no gray, no hair loss, no wrinkles except those of facial expression. He moved easily, lithely. Jemison Thorsby was studying him now as a rabbit stares at a stalking Bobcat. As they moved together, a few steps farther..., he was sure. This could not be an old man who just happened to look younger. The pilot was assuredly, undeniably, young. Besides..., now finally the thought swept over him...how odd it was that a flyer should land a plane, strike up conversation with a complete stranger. The certainty of it settled over him like a chilling wind! There was a puzzling strangeness here, a thing bewildering, bizarre.

"One night..., during that summer camp in 1949," his tone was wracked with question, voice stiff with unease ...perceiving, perhaps, a connection, "we lost a P-51 and the pilot in a crash."

"July 26, 1949," the pilot said it quietly, leaning against the wing, features more serious, pained. "It happens so fast. One minute you're the best in the world. The next...?" he shrugged. "You go over it again and again trying to figure how you could let it go so wrong...!"

Apprehension!...No!...Far more!...Stark fear! erupted, barreled through his being. His eyes riveted, searched deep into the pale green eyes before him. "The lieutenant who headed our radio unit was the pilot's best friend. He was gone when reveille woke us that morning, when we heard about...about...the... the crash. He left during the night...went back to Birmingham to tell the pilot's wife about his...about the..."

"Parsons," the pilot interrupted him, soft spoken, pensive now. "Old Parsons. He was there when I...when we needed him. Six foot four, dark curly hair, big grin, really handsome guy. Yeah. He was my best friend."

"You...," words quavered, faltered in bewilderment, disbelief. But then, who else would know..., could possibly know those things? Panic swept over him, panic so tight, so hard he thought for a second he couldn't breathe. His eyes darted left, right, like a hobo with his foot caught in a rail, frozen in the headlights of an oncoming train... his mind bounding like a running deer, frantically searching for the way out. The ache to flee, to race away became acute, an energy drawn in upon itself. "The pilot that night...," his voice withered, stretched taut with fear, foreboding, "it was ...was you who..., who..."

In the same breath came a curious, minuscule, gnawing of equilibrium, of cognizance, of submission. Where, after all, could he run? They were alone, miles from another human being, from aid of any kind. There could be no easy way, no quick escape. The knowing rose up from deep inside that there was nothing left but to confront, to endure, to experience whatever this was before him. Yet his fear was visible, a radiating, palpable thing.

The pilot raised a hand, palm outward, open, long the unspoken sign of peace among the diverse throng of humanity.

"Wait...," the words were commanding, yet softly spoken. "Please. Don't be afraid...," his smile was gentle, "...it's all right."

In the pale green depths of the pilot's eyes he could see the well of kindness, assurance. And as he looked the pilot's form, his flight suit, his battered leather jacket and hat, his hands, the features of his face, became incandescent, misty with shimmering light. It was a light that glowed brightly even in the strength of the morning sun.

Suddenly, in the midst of terrible fear, came the tiniest core of assurance. Somehow, in a way far from his own understanding, it could be, might well be, all right.

Words surged, then, into his consciousness, words from a Christmastime in the years of his childhood. How old had he been...eleven, twelve...? ...when he'd memorized his role in the Christmas pageant? The words were few, but they were taken from an entire text he repeated from memory every Christmas Eve, just to see that he could remember the words, the shepherds...

"...an Angel of the Lord came upon them, and the
Glory of the Lord shone round about them, and they
were sore afraid! But the Angel said 'fear not'..."

He'd wondered idly, over the years, why modern man could no longer share the miracles, see the Angels. He'd often wondered, too, how those shepherds had dealt with the stunning fear of such an unexpected, unbelievable sight. Among familiar words, the wonder of ancient herds men he found a mustard seed of composure, of growing curiosity. Frozen moments ticked by as he stood mute, collecting himself, searching the pilot's face, measuring reality, sanity, acceptance of a thing no one, in human terms, could fully understand.

When finally he could speak it was without

question, matter of fact. Instinctively he sensed that easing calm, a prodding of acceptance, could in no way be fully of his own making.

"You were the pilot," he said at last, "the one we lost here that night in 1949."

The pilot grinned. Then more broadly, the grin expanding into laughter, unconstrained, hearty. He was himself again, the glow gone. "OK, pal, you finally figured it out," his laughter stretched long. "Thank goodness! The suspense was killing me!"

"So you're a...," hesitant yet, fearful to say the word, to acknowledge the unbelievable, "...a... ghost...?"

The pilot laughed again. "To be honest, pal, we like the word Angel. Sounds better, ya' know. Not so menacing."

"So this...I mean...our...our meeting here today...it's not just by...by chance?" this time it was a question.

The Angel shook his head. "Right you are, old buddy, I knew you'd be here," he poked a finger toward him, grin still livening his face. "Thought, maybe, I could take you for a ride," his hand made a sweeping gesture toward the plane. "Even better, how 'bout you fly...and I'll ride with you."

Confusion shadowed his face. How could the pilot, the Angel, know? Even he had not known he was coming to the old abandoned air base until he started the car that morning.

The suggestion jarred him swiftly out of wondering. "Wait...," his objection was instant, hands raised in a barrier of protest, "I can't fly that thing!"

"Why not? You know a lot about it," the Angel chuckled, "you've flown before."

"Sure, quite a bit..., but...," in a tiny less-busy corner of his mind he wondered how the Angel knew that.

"You've been at the controls, know how they work?"

"Well...A good many times. I've flown quite a few hours, made take-offs, flown the pattern, made landing approaches. Those were small planes, nothing like a Mustang," he in turn gestured toward the sleek fighter. "I couldn't handle a plane like this!"

"You'll be surprised," the Angel assured, "sure, it's faster, heavier. But that makes it steadier, too. Doesn't bounce around as much. Plenty of power. Lots of ways, it's easier once you get the hang of it."

"I've never really completed a landing." He said it thoughtfully, curious now, glancing longingly at the plane. "How would I get it down again?"

"I'll be right there, show you how, be on the controls with you when you need it," the Angel spoke with quiet certainty, his voice earnest, reassuring. The sunny smile reappeared, "Don't worry. We'll get you back in one piece, pal!"

"I wonder...," his sentence dangled, hanging in the air like a magic rope, his mind weighing risk against the power of a lifelong dream.

"...I'll bet I could get it up there...," he said it half-aloud, more to himself than to the Angel.

Thoughts tumbled quickly. His children were grown, successful, on their own. Though they were far from wealthy, his wife would be okay financially if...if...?

And...if he crashed, wasn't his life..., well his future at least, about over anyway? He reached, gripped the metal of the wing, yet cold from high flight, testing its hardness, reassuring himself of it's reality.

"It's real, solid as a rock, as long as you're on board," the Angel's laugh was quiet, understanding. "You know, pal, not many of us, while we're down here, get a chance to do the impossible, to see a bit beyond, to understand a little more."

"It's hard to argue with that," Thorsby mused.

"In a way, I guess, it'd be crazy not to..." Unmistakable was a sense that the decision was not his alone, that to go had become an essential part of whatever was left of his life.

CHAPTER FOUR

"WHAT THE HECK!," he said it suddenly, impulsively. "Why not...?" He stepped around the Angel to the plane's fuselage, pushed into hidden hinged panels that revealed step, handhold, and climbed up onto the wing. As his eyes came level with the cockpit he saw the name stenciled under the canopy '1st Lt. Robert M. "Rob",...The last name was simple, a bit unusual, one he'd seldom seen. He began to spell it in his mind 'A..d...d...i...s...o...n.'

"Hold it, I've got a flight suit for you," the Angel's voice interrupted his train of thought. "A hat, too." The Angel keyed open a small hatch in the side of the plane's fuselage and tossed them onto the wing next to the parachute. "Use the chute there on the wing."

He pondered it for a moment more as he kicked off penny loafers, stepped into legs of the flight suit, pulled it shoulder high, slipped arms in, zipped it up, donned shoes again. The suit was fitted for him...or someone exactly his size. The hat fit just as perfectly. Whatever this encounter was, it's happening was meant for him. There was awe in that, wonder, anxiety, budding hope that it might be all right.

When he slipped the straps over his shoulders the bulk of the chute bumped clumsily behind his knees. For that reason flyers seldom wear a seat pack parachute until ready to board. The feel of it was familiar from decades before when he had flown with the Angel's fellow bomber pilots from the Birmingham airfield.

"Let me get back here before you get in," the Angel tilted the seat forward and climbed into a small canvas seat behind the cockpit. "Not many P-51's have two seats, but this 'K' model does. OK, pal, climb aboard."

He stepped over the cockpit side into the curved metal of the bucket seat, nearly crushing a pale blue card under his foot. Intent on what he was doing, he picked the card up, hurriedly slipping it inside the flight suit into his shirt pocket, and slid down into the seat. The chute under him became a cushion lifting him to proper visibility through the three glass panels of the wind-screen.

From the ground the P-51 is lean, sleek, graceful. In the cockpit, over the wide spread of the wings, behind the bulk of the long, high pitched, engine nacelle the plane appeared heavy, clumsy at first. Pangs of un-ease crawled in his gut. It was the stark newness of the ancient aircraft that riveted his attention away from anxiety.

What was it the Angel had said..., "where I am everything is new"...? The old plane not only gleamed with newness, there was the scent of it also, the smell of new bakelite instrument mountings, new electrical equipment, new paint. The pungent odor of hot oil and high octane aviation gasoline permeated the cockpit. Instruments and instruction cards were spotless, easy to read.

His right hand palmed the control stick between his knees, left hand cupped the black rubber-coated throttle, so much like the business end of a bicycle handlebar. His feet mounted rudder-brake pedals under the instrument panel.

Compared to the dazzling technical array in modern jets the P-51's instruments seemed simple, straight forward, easy to identify and understand. Right hand on the control stick, all other controls near the left. His feet felt constrained at first, separated by instruments and controls, stuck into short tunnels, pedals wider than expected, heavy.

"Lets see," he mused to the Angel, "this is the prop control, this the carburetor heat control," he touched each as he named it, "the mixture control, the landing flap lever..."

"Wait,...no," the Angel interjected, "that's the landing gear handle. Back here, near the seat, that's the flap control."

"Got it! Thanks," he grinned, glancing back toward the Angel. "Here's the air speed indicator, the turn and bank indicator, the rate of climb indicator, the altimeter, the RPM indicator, manifold pressure, engine temperature, oil pressure..."

"Kind of amazing," the Angel clapped him on the shoulder. "See how much you know?...and not even licensed! This oughta be easier than we thought."

He memorized the location of vital controls and instruments, repeatedly drilled by the Angel, surprised when more than an hour had slipped by.

"Okay!" The Angel gave him a friendly whack on the shoulder again. "Lets fire her up." Out of nowhere, near the wing, two sergeants appeared manning a bulky red fire extinguisher mounted on large black metal wheels.

"Clear?" the Angel yelled out to them.

"All clear," came their answer.

"Master switch on, mixture control full rich, magneto switch on 'both'." His fingers reached at the Angels command. "Starter energiser." The sound of the inertial starter began with a gravelly moan, rising rapidly as its heavy flywheel gathered speed. "Engage," the Angel ordered as its whine crested at a shrill pitch. At the flip of the switch the huge prop blades wind-milled slowly, lazily. Suddenly, with staccato blare the big engine caught, belching puffs of light blue smoke as twelve cylinders exploded into life. The plane shuddered, it's big propellor thrust into a blur. Strong blasts of propwash danced suddenly around the open cockpit canopy. The two sergeants backed away from the plane, dragging the fire extinguisher cart. They snapped to attention, saluted,...vanished as quickly as they had appeared.

"Great, pal, we got 'er goin'," he was surprised that he could hear the Angel's voice so easily over the roar of the engine. "Lets taxi around, get the feel of 'er."

He moved the throttle bar forward, feeling the engine surge, kahki sleeves of his flight suit rippling in gusts from the big prop. The P-51 rolled easily. He pressed the tops of the rudder pedals with the toes of his penny loafers, applying left brake, then right, bringing the plane to a stop.

He applied power again rolling forward, stopping, revving the big Rolls-Royce Merlin, steering round and round the empty tarmac. For nearly half an hour he taxied the plane, reveling in the power of the engine, checking instruments, getting the feel of controls. The plane was smooth, responsive to his touch. He was surprised at how quickly he felt a part of it, finally at least a bit comfortable that he - with the Angel's help of course - might be able to put it where he wanted it to go.

"Okay, pal, you're doin' great," the Angel's voice was loud in his ear. "Lets go take a look at the runway." He revved the engine, touched the left brake, spun the P-51 in a tight half circle and headed toward the taxi strip weaving left and right so he could see ahead past the long high-set engine nacelle. At the bend in the taxi strip, a touch of the right toe brake, full right rudder, brought them smoothly around the turn. Under his guidance, the plane, weaving, rocking gently over old uneven asphalt, rolled the couple of hundred yards to the runway's edge.

CHAPTER FIVE

"LET'S DO THE FINAL engine check," the Angel spoke as soon as Thorsby brought the plane to a stop. "Put the earphones on, it'll protect your ears some from the noise. Radio is on the Eglin control channel."

At the Angel's direction he advanced throttle to full power switching to left then right magneto to assure correct performance. Together they checked engine RPM, temperature, oil pressure, until the Angel said, "everything's in the green, bring it back to idle." The roar of the engine dropped to a purr as he pulled the throttle bar back.

"You can't see me up there, but here's how I'll help when you need it," the voice came over his shoulder. The Angel, he knew, had no controls in the back seat, but the rudder pedals and control stick moved firmly, without pressure from his own hands or feet. How does he do that, he wondered? The throttle advanced, the plane rolled forward onto the runway, turned, aimed down the middle of it as though of it's own volition.

"You better tell Eglin control we're here. They can see us now you're onboard. The identification number for our plane is 472811. Just use the last three numbers, 811."

He thumbed the send button, glanced at his wristwatch, saw that it was still a few minutes before nine, spoke self-consciously into the microphone. "Uhh, Eglin control this is Alabama Air National Guard 811, ready for take-off from auxiliary field one."

The earphones crackled with static, "Roger, 811, this is Eglin control. Uhhh, hold a minute 811."

"Tell 'em," the Angel leaned close behind him, "we came south down the civilian corridor, forgot to check in."

"Uhhh, 811, this is Eglin control. We have no check-in, no report of you in our airspace."

"Roger, Eglin control, we came down the civilian corridor, turned in to here. Forgot to check in with you. Sorry."

"811, we have no record of you on radar."

"Roger, Eglin. We came down a couple of hours ago. Are you having some radar problems?"

The Angel howled with laughter behind him. "Way to go, pal," he said, whacking his shoulder gleefully, "blame it on them, works every time in this man's army."

"Uhh, 811, it has been a little busy, we'll go ahead and clear you for takeoff and note that you're active in our airspace. Remember you have no control tower there. You're on your own for takeoff and climb out. Check with us when you're airborne. Eglin control standing by."

The voice behind him was still shaking with laughter, "See what I mean? Okay, pal, she's all yours. Shut the canopy and tell 'em we're rolling."

Reaching for the crank on his right, just below and at the forward edge of the canopy, he rotated the black wooden handle until the plexiglas bubble slid firmly closed over them. "Thanks, Eglin," into the mike. "We'll report when airborne. 811 rolling."

"Hold the stick all the way back so that big prop doesn't hit the runway," the Angel cautioned. "Then just ease up on it 'til the tail comes off the ground."

"Got it," he palmed the throttle forward, released toe brakes. The P-51 began to roll. More throttle, vibration from the engine's power hummed in the plane's metal skin, instruments, controls. Full power! Lots of rudder to hold it straight against the pull of the big prop's torque. Roar from the engine was overwhelming even with the canopy closed. Speed 20, 30, 40, 50 miles per hour, he eased the stick forward, oh-so-carefully.

"Easy! Easy! That's it! Hold it...hold it!" the Angel's voice was tense, mothering. "There...just right!"

The tail lifted. At last, he could see ahead, over the long engine nacelle, through the rectangular center panel of the wind screen as he gathered speed ...60, 70 mph. The heavy, clumsy feeling vanished. Instead, the plane felt as light as the air streaming around it, instantly responsive, balanced as gracefully as a ballerina on the two main wheels of the landing gear, tail surfaces already floating in the blast from the blurred arc of the eleven foot propellor.

80, 90 mph! They crested a low rise, raced down the gentle slope beyond, asphalt under the spinning tires a rushing torrent of gray, growing swiftly shorter ahead, disappearing under the tail wheel. The howling roar of the engine, throbbing at full power hurled them toward a wall of green and brown. Pine trees, ramrod straight, blue sky tall, dashed madly toward them, towering larger by the second in the wind-screen's center panel.

"Hold it there, pal," he could feel the Angel leaning forward behind him, peering over his shoulder, words quick, eager, "we'll ease her off about 120."

100, 110 mph! He reached down to his left near the cockpit floor, gripped the landing gear lever, eyes flicking from airspeed indicator to runway's end, to the green wall just beyond, rushing toward them.

120 mph. Stick back...ever-so-gently! Subtle movement left, right, a fluid drifting, floating, unfettered now, parting from earth's umbilical, the gushing river of runway. Freed from frenzied roll to be borne by the rushing wind, transfigured from racing panther to fleet falcon. He was peering intently now, fascinated, at the middle of the tree barrier instead of its roots.

"Gear up," he pulled the gear lever at the sound of the voice behind him, nudged the stick back toward his gut. "Easy, easy, not too much," the Angel cautioned. The wall of trees sank below the blur of the whirling prop. 130 mph! The whine of hydraulics, muted by the engine's howl, nested landing gear into the plane's belly. He felt the plane shudder as wheels thumped into place, heard the squeal of rushing air as the last cracks in the gear doors were sucked into streamlined position.

140 mph. The wall of green exploded past, a bare hundred feet under his wings.

"Yahooooo!!," he yelled as the forest cascaded beneath him, a surging ocean of green leaves, brown bark, tall trees, stunted ones, clearings, green grass and gold, sun glinting off blue ponds, flowing, racing under the cutting edge of his wings. Muted laughter came again from the back seat.

Stick back a bit more, gray blur of the big whirling prop pointing higher, toward the pale blue of the sky. "Okay, throttle back." He palmed the round rubber-covered bar back at the Angel's command. "A little more...little more, that's it! We'll climb out at about 75% power." The straining full-power howl of the engine faded to a sweet throbbing drone. Left hand down, back, near the rear of the seat, flap control handle to the 'up' position. He glanced over his shoulders at the back edge of the wings checking to see that the landing flaps came up, streamlined.

Freed from drag of landing gear and flaps, the plane slipping slickly through the air, he eased the stick back farther, pointing the whirling prop higher into the light blue of the sky. The forest dropped quickly away beneath his wings as the P-51 ballooned upward at 1500 feet a minute. He pressed the stick left, nudged the left rudder, guiding the plane into a climbing turn, the forest wheeling below, until, over steeply banked wing, he could see the remnants of Auxiliary Field #1 from far above.

"Well done, good buddy, I didn't have to help much with that part," came the voice from the back seat. "Let's level off about 3,000. Throttle back. That's it, a little more, little more. Good! About 40% power. We'll cruise around at 170 or so, let you get the feel of 'er. Better tell 'em we're up here, pal," the Angel reminded. "Tell 'em we're gonna be in this sector."

"Thanks, I forgot," he keyed the mike, continuing to circle the field. "Eglin, this is Air Guard 811. Airborne. We'll be running practice maneuvers in the Auxiliary Field One sector. Will clear with you when we move. Over."

"Roger 811, this is Eglin control. Acknowledged. Reporting you near Auxiliary one. We'll stand by. Eglin out."

"811 out."

"Okay, pal, lets put 'er through the paces," he could feel the Angel leaning toward him again.

With the voice at his back he guided the plane in shallow turns, steep ones, circles, weaving back and forth over the straight line of the Bob Sikes Road, climbing, gliding. He was surprised when he realized a half hour had passed. "Okay, I think you've got the idea," the Angel moved them on. "Ya' know, pal, you've got some talent for this. You always felt you could do it, didn't you?"

"Yeah...," his smile was still far from relaxed.

"...Guess I did,"

"Lets take 'er upstairs, show you a couple of other little things," the Angel's voice was fervent over his shoulder. "Throttle up to about 85% power. Let 'er run to 275, she'll climb fast from that speed."

The P-51 charged ahead, near full throttle, quickly surpassing 200, 220, 240, 260 miles per hour, 3,000 feet above the forest. At 275 mph he pulled the stick back toward his belt again, gray blur of the big prop clawing upward into the pale blue of the sky, the plane climbing, soaring at 3,000 feet per minute. "Hot dang," he sang out, "this baby climbs like a homesick angel!"

Silence from the back seat...except for a hesitant clearing of the Angel's throat.

"Sorry," there was little time for embarrassment, "I didn't mean..."

"Forget it pal," laughter came again to the Angel's voice. "You're right, she does climb like a homesick angel. We're coming through 7,000. Level 'er off at 8,000. Bring 'er back to half throttle. That'll give us about 200."

They were at 8,300 feet before he could level off, throttle back, airspeed at 205 mph. The air coming in the cockpit vent was cooler, thin, crisp.

"Line 'er up with the road again," the Angel directed. He guided the P-51 around to the road, headed west above the ribbon of asphalt. The deserted little base, far below, ahead to their left, was visible through the clear bubble of the canopy. "Okay, pal lets do a slow roll to the left."

"Do a what?," incredulously. He knew very well what the Angel meant.

"You can do it, pal," the Angel said. "By the numbers. One, nose up just a hair so we're floating upward slightly to hold altitude. Two, roll to the left, point the wing at the ground. Three, on your back rolling on over. Four, coming over, right wing pointing at the ground. Five, right side up again. Easy as pie."

"Says you," he swallowed hard, but hesitated only a few seconds. "Well, here we go," he nudged the stick back, actions and thoughts merging. Nose up just a little, stick left, wing roll-

ing, deep down. Feels like we'll fall off, crash...
whoa!... rolling... all the way over, world upside
down! Hey, will we fall out?... ohh, thank God...
we're coming over, around... right wing pointing
at the ground, coming up, up, up, up...level, right-
side up again! "Good grief, makes you kinda
dizzy, doesn't it?"

Laughter again from the back seat. The Angel whacked him on the shoulder gleefully, "Way
to go, pal. Couldn't have done it better myself.
The idea is to stare straight ahead along the top
of the engine, watch the ground out of the corner
of your eyes, a tiny pause at each point of the
roll. Keeps you from gettin' dizzy. Lets do it again."

"Whooo boy...!," he muttered, nudging the
stick back again. When the world had rolled
around them, and they were on top of it again,
they had come to the end of the Bob Sikes Road,
the place where it dead-ends into the Mossyhead
Highway. He banked hard to the right, then a
steep, tight full circle to the left, to head east over
the gray ribbon of the old road again. By the tenth
roll he'd forgotten the dizziness. The slow lazy
turn of earth around, up-side-down, overhead,
seemed less strange each time. The feeling of
proficiency, of skill, was a satisfying thing.

"Let's try a loop," enthusiasm edged the

47

Angel's voice. "I'll just talk you right through this one." In a very real sense he flew guiding words from the back seat. When the needle on the airspeed indicator surged past 250 mph, throttle full open, he eased back firmly on the stick, lifting the nose sharply, up, steeper, straight up, prop clutching at the air, plane slowing against the drag of gravity, over, farther, upside down, world above his head, haunches rammed up into the seat by the centrifugal force of the plane's arc.

Around the backside of the loop, nosing down again, throttling back so as not to gain too much speed, falling, curving back toward the green-brown earth, diving, down, straight down, earth filling the windscreen, nose lifting, up, up, up, aahhh!, back to level flight again, throttle forward to cruise speed, stomach churning.

"We lost 500 feet on that one," the Angel's voice was matter-of-fact, not critical. "This time, try to hold the stick in a fixed position all the way through the loop. She'll come out about where you started."

8,000 feet above the old, barren, auxiliary airbase, he flew the loop again and again until there were the beginnings of familiarity, even perhaps, a bit of comfort. They merged the slow roll and loop into an Immelman turn, looping upward until the plane was upside down, rolling quickly over at the top of the loop, heading the opposite way several hundred feet higher. A reverse Immelmann rolls the plane over onto it's back, dives down through the second half of a loop, ends heading the opposite way several hundred feet lower.

Those dances in the air...surging climb, dive, turn, circle, loop, roll, climbing turn, diving turn, Immelmann turn, reverse Immelmann are the core of the fighter pilot's bag of tricks in an aerial dogfight, the one-on-one struggle to destroy, or to stay alive.

"Way to go, old buddy," the Angel gave his shoulder a congratulatory thump. "I wish I'd gotten the feel of it as quick. Lets go down and try a few landings." With the Angel's instruction he pulled the throttle back to near idle, nudged forward on the stick putting the P-51 into a shallow glide back toward the little base. Carburetor ice build-up is a danger when engine power is greatly reduced, so he turned on full carburetor heat to protect the engine, keep it running. With engine near idle the eleven foot arc of the four-bladed propellor dragged against air like a brake, letting them descend steeply, quickly, while maintaining moderate speed. The big prop, resisting the plane's natural bent to gain speed in the dive made a paddling sound as it wind-milled lazily against the wind rush, and the craft shuddered in rhythm with it.

"Pal, how 'bout a mid-morning snack?" with the voice from the back seat came the sound of paper rattling and the clink of glass.

"Yeah, my stomach thinks my throat's been cut. Forgot to eat breakfast." He muttered the stale old adage impulsively as the Angel pushed a small, cold bottle and a brown paper bag over his shoulder. Holding the stick with his knees he opened the bag. "Hey, Ritz crackers and peanut butter, one of my favorite things in the whole world. And look at this! Grapette! Man, I haven't had one of these in years. I used to drink 'em all the time when I was a teenager in Georgia."

"I've never seen 'em outside the Deep South. They had 'em in Alabama where I grew up, too," the Angel expounded. "There's just no grape drink that tastes as good,"

"Yeah. Isn't it funny how Northerners call soft drinks 'pop' or 'soda'. Down here we call 'em what they are, 'cold drinks'."

"Whoever said they know how to live up there, anyway?," the Angel replied. They laughed to-gether at the Southern joke, eating double crackers with thick slabs of crunchy peanut butter between, washing them down with swigs of Grapette.

"Did you know...?" he turned his head, spoke over his shoulder to the Angel, "General Jimmy Doolittle and his crews practiced for that famous World War II raid over Tokyo here at old Auxiliary #1 in 1942?"

"No kidding?," the Angel responded. "Gosh, that was some mission. Can you imagine a heavy twin-engine B-25 bomber taking off from the short deck of an aircraft carrier? Makes you wonder how they did it."

"Well, they learned to do it right down there," he pointed down at the empty little base, drifting closer now, forgotten since those glory years. "President Franklin D. Roosevelt never told the name of that aircraft carrier. He just called it Shangri-La. I guess old Auxiliary Field #1 is Shangri-La, too. At least, a part of Shangri-La, anyway."

"How 'bout that," the Angel chuckled, "we're flyin' out of a field that has a place in world history, only nobody knows it but us."

"Maybe all that counts anymore is that we know it. Things change. Life happens and moves on, I guess," he didn't laugh. It sounded too much like his own life at that moment. In the few minutes it took the plane to slide quietly down from above 8,000 feet he ate more than a dozen of the doubled crackers stuck together with rich slabs of crunchy peanut butter and swigged down two bottles of the sweet grape drink.

As they drifted nearer the earth he guided the plane in a shallow turn toward the field, sinking to a thousand feet, flying wide of but along the runway opposite from takeoff, the downwind leg of the landing pattern.

"Okay, pal, throttle up to hold at 130, leave the carburetor heat on, carburetor mixture control to 'full rich', flaps down 25%."

"Got it," he said after the few seconds it took to adjust those controls. "Gear coming down," he pushed the lever forward. The gear warning light glowed green, indicating gear down, locked.

"Good man," the Angel said. "Lets roll back the canopy and go in open cockpit." The cockpit canopy slid open as he turned the crank and the 130 mile per hour wind rush roared, buffeted, whistled around them. He flew the length of the runway, past it's end, beyond the Bob Sikes Road. At the Angel's direction, he banked steeply into a sharp left turn onto the base leg of the landing pattern. A few seconds later another steeply banked left turn onto final approach guided the plane toward the gray slash of the runway looming through the blurred arc of the prop.

"Full flaps," the Angel commanded, "throttle back a bit more. I usually come in on final at 115 but lets hold 120. Gives us a safety edge."

He eased the throttle back, touched the stick forward, aimed the whirling prop downward at mottled grass short of the runway edge, airspeed down to 125, 115, 110, "oops!...", throttle forward just a hair, steady at 120 miles per hour. From a mile away and a thousand feet high the runway looked postage stamp size... scary, too narrow, too short. At 800 feet the P-51 began to bump, wallow in near-ground air currents. Straining to keep the runway centered above the long engine nacelle, his feet danced side to side on rudder pedals, hands jockeyed the stick forward, back, left, right. The runway seemed an impossible target, sliding back and forth, up and down around the nose of the plane. At slower speed the controls felt so different, sloppy, heavy, slower to respond, needing greater movement, a last minute frantic re-learning as the runway approached.

"Relax, pal! Flow with it!" he felt the Angel nudge the controls with him. "Let it bounce around. Just keep it aimed near the end of the runway. When we get closer, you can see it's wide enough, then aim for the center."

500 feet, half a mile out, he fought the controls of the bouncing, wallowing plane, straining to hold it straight. The runway loomed wider, longer. Just when he thought he was near losing control, the bouncing and wallowing began to ease. At 200 feet and a quarter of a mile the runway gaped wide, a 5,000 foot gash in the green of the forest, its center a broad target.

Forest behind, now...grass underneath the front edge of the wings. 100 feet. Back on the stick, nose up just a little. 50 feet. Flare out, throttle back. Float. Float. Speed down to 110, asphalt rushing toward him. The runway threshold flashed past, the paving again a river of gray racing beneath the wings. He held it straight, let it float, 100 mph, stick back a little more. The plane sank slowly in the wind rush, his feet fighting the rudder pedals, the plane's nose wavering left, right. He heard the screech as tires kissed the runway. Twin puffs of hot blue smoke from tortured rubber gusted past the back edge of the wing. The plane lurched upward, floated in the whistle of fast moving air, settled again to the runway. Mismatched squeals barked from each side as tires thumped to the pavement unevenly, blue puffs swirling under the wings. The plane bounced from side to side, quieted, rolled firmly, safely on the ground. Its tail wheel sank slowly to the runway. "Oh, man!," he muttered, hastily daubing beads of sweat from his brow with the back of his hand.

With tail wheel down the long engine nacelle blocked forward vision again. Peering through triangular side panes of the windscreen he tracked the runway's edge to guide straight while he braked the still rushing plane with the toes of penny loafers.

"Full throttle! Full throttle! Lets go around again!" the voice sang from the back seat.

"Oh, Darn!" Nerves wired tight as shoelaces, he eased the throttle forward. "Sorry about that!" he mumbled hurriedly as the fighter hurtled forward again.

CHAPTER SIX

IT WAS NOT UNTIL the fourth landing that he began to feel easier, to breathe almost normally as the runway rushed up to meet him. Lifting off again after the sixth landing, he began to feel the first breath of confidence that he could put the P-51 on the ground, far from perfectly, of course...but, perhaps at least, in one piece.

"Okay, pal, lets go buzz the beaches," he could feel the Angel leaning forward behind him. Landing gear thumped into the belly of the plane, flaps whined into streamlined position. He pointed the right wing toward the ground, banked the plane into a climbing turn and aimed the whirling arc of the prop toward the thin blue line of ocean on the horizon to the south.

"Hey!...Wait!...Look!...Three o'clock, low!" the Angel's voice was abrupt, hurried. In World War II aviation parlance, direction was referred to as though the plane was on the face of a clock with the nose pointing to twelve. 'Three o'clock, low' was to the right, below the wing.

"On the ground. Three targets. That truck is

leavin' in a hurry. There's gonna be a firing run."
There was a level of excitement in the Angel's
voice, unheard before. Pressure on the stick and
rudder pedals overrode his control, banking the
P-51 more steeply, drawing the plane tighter into
the turn. Below the right wing, an airplane and
two military vehicles were in a long forest clearing, two of them positioned in squares of white,
obviously immediate targets.

"An old North American B-26 'Invader'
bomber, and an old Patton tank." He described
them over his shoulder to the Angel.

"Yeah! You got a good eye, pal." the Angel's
tone was still hurried. "There's a couple more of
each sittin' between trees about a thousand feet
to the left. That old six-by truck about six or eight
hundred feet to the right looks like it's abandoned.
Really rusty. Not marked as a target." The target
area slid past under them. "Break left, pal, hard
left. Give it more power. Hold altitude. Where are
we, about fourteen hundred feet?"

"Yeah, 1350," he glanced at the altimeter as
he banked the fighter into a steep turn to the left.
The dark blue military truck came into his view
speeding away from the target area along a red
clay road, a rooster tail of ruddy dust rising
behind it.

"Hot dog, I haven't been able to shoot these things for forty years," the Angel's excitement rose. "With you on board the ammo is hard again. Flip the gun arming switch."

"What?"

"There. To your left. On the little panel under the throttle. Yeah, that's it. Flip the red cover up. Now push the switch." A small red light glowed red on the instrument panel.

"Are you sure we oughta do this? Don't we need clearance or something to fire these guns?"

"We don't wanna mess up their targets, pal. We'll just put a few rounds into that rusty old truck to the right. It's a goner anyway. Looks like its been there since Nero was a pup. Why would anybody care about a few bullet holes in that thing?"

"I don't know...? They're kind of picky about the base these days. Not like wartime."

"Hard left! Quick! Before they get here! Come around 180 degrees and head back."

The left wing pointed at the ground as he banked the plane steeply into a tight left turn. The forest wheeled below until he rolled level again, target area ahead in the blur of the prop.

"Okay, pal, we're about two and a half miles out. Gives us time to line up. We've probably got time for one run. Can you see through the gunsight?"

"Yeah, seems to be clear." The gunsight was above the instrument panel, behind the forward panel of the windscreen.

"Center your target in it, along the top of the engine nacelle. Think of the whole plane as a rifle, just point the spinner on the prop at the truck."

"Is this the gun trigger, here on the stick?," the target area was sweeping toward them.

"Right under your finger, pal. Don't squeeze it until I tell you. See that tall dead pine tree ahead?"

"Yeah, just to the right a little." The tree towered over others, a brown splash in a sea of green leaves.

"It's about a mile out. We'll start our run there, aim down at the target. We're doin' 220, should be at about 270 when we pull up. Good! Leave the throttle setting where it is," the Angel's voice was edged with excitement.

There was no time for reply, it all happened too fast. His heart beat faster, palms clammy as the dead tree rushed past under their wings. He nudged the stick forward, jockeyed the rudder pedals with his feet, brought the old rusty truck dead ahead, over the engine nacelle.

"Okay, pal, give it several two second bursts when I tell you. You'll see the dust fly. Walk it up to the truck, hold right on it, give it a long one."

"Are you sure we....?"

"Shoot, dammit!" The plane seemed to stagger, slow in the air as six fifty caliber machine guns, three in each wing, exploded into deafening din. Light blue smoke surged around gun barrels in the wing's leading edge, flowed in the air-stream back over the wings. Occasional fingers of fire, tracer bullets to mark the path, streaked toward the ground. Dust puffs, like hard raindrops on a pond, leaped on the ground far ahead of the plane, dancing toward the truck. The truck, the leaping little raindrops of dust, rushed toward his gunsight. The tops of trees raced wildly under them as they angled closer to earth, faster, faster.

Dancing dust tiptoed up to the truck, became winking fireflies as bullets exploded into metal, then over, beyond. He pressed the stick forward, guided the ripping bullets back into the truck and gave the chattering machine guns a long burst.

It was astoundingly sudden! Totally unexpected! The enormous bright flash, the surging ring of concussion mist, the truck dissolving, disappearing, bit's and pieces hurled outward, upward, with the blast. A roiling, mushrooming column of smoke, black, menacing, ballooned, billowing high in front of the whirling prop.

"Up!...Break left!...Hard!" the Angel's words were a shout! Instantly he was with Thorsby on the controls, added pressure on his hands and feet. The fighter surged suddenly upward, bank deeply, hard, to the left, almost upside down. The weight of centrifugal force rammed him into the seat, cheeks sagged, jaw forced open with the tight fast turn. He flicked an eye toward the airspeed indicator. Almost three hundred. The plane snapped over to the opposite side in a climbing turn to the right, a bit more gently, to circle the astonishing explosion. At the top of the roiling black column of smoke the metal roof of the truck cab, ripped from it's supports by the blast, rolled lazily, hung, momentarily suspended in the air before sinking downward, gaining speed, plunging back to earth.

"What the hell was that...?," Thorsby leveled off at 3,500 feet, reduced power, still circling the rising tower of black cloud. There was silence from the back seat as they glanced over the plane and instruments for possible damage.

"I guess," the Angel's tone was subdued, sheepish, "they must have been using the old truck to store explosives. Probably using 'em to make hit's on the other targets a little more realistic."

"We didn't need it to be that realistic!" Thorsby meant it as humor. There was no laughter from the back seat. The Angel was silent as he rolled out of the turn, headed south toward the ocean, away from the towering smoke. His eye caught a glimmer of rapid movement. "Here he comes," he jerked a thumb downward. Behind the left wing a jet fighter streaked above the forest toward the target area 3,000 feet below them.

"Holy smoke!...he must be doin' near 600 miles an hour," the Angel's voice was filled with awe.

"Yeah, those F-16's really move," he banked the P-51 into a steep, hard, right turn so they could look back at the target area. Two fingers of fire, one from under each wing of the jet, slashed toward the targets. A second later two more followed. Twin blasts rocked the tank and the plane as rockets exploded into both of them. Columns of black smoke much smaller than the one from the old truck boiled up into the air.

"Man!...he killed both targets in the same

pass," the Angel's voice was sharp with excitement as they watched the sleek jet fighter arc sharply upward, blast past, soar far above them, arrowing straight up, out of sight . "Whoooo!! Those young guys are so lucky to fly a plane like that!"

"You'll probably get a close-up look in a few seconds," he said over his shoulder to the Angel. "That pilot must be asking why there was a hit near the targets before he got there." He banked the P-51 to the south again. The blue expanse of the Gulf of Mexico and the glistening white of the shore drifted closer.

"The guys in the truck were around a bend in the clay road," he continued. "I don't think they saw who blew the truck, but they know we're up here. They must have a radio. You can bet Eglin will vector that jet to look us over."

"Change to the emergency channel. Lets see if we can hear them," the Angel's voice was hurried. "Here let me do it." On the third radio channel they tried, voices crackled into the earphones.

"Red Leader One, this is Eglin. The unidentified aircraft is nearing the shoreline just east of Hurlburt Field, about 160 degrees from you."

"Roger, Eglin, I've got a radar lock-on. We'll go have a look."

63

Chapter Seven

As HE DRIFTED SOUTHWARD toward the shore a scant 800 feet over the growing clusters of houses, roads, streets, the habitation of modest seaside towns he slowed the P-51 to 140 miles an hour. "That guy will struggle like heck to keep an F-16 this slow," he chuckled easing landing flaps down 15% to stabilize the plane at that lazy - for a fighter - speed.

As he flew over, and well past, Shalimar and it's brief bridge...to his right, through the wide bubble of the plane's canopy, Thorsby could see the long runway at Hurlburt Air Force Base. He realized that 800 feet would also be near pattern altitude for landing planes. Sharply, deeply banking, twisting the P-51 hard left, then right, glancing behind...sure enough... there was a big four engine C-130 trailing them.

In fact, Thorsby knew the big plane's speed would be hardly more than theirs in its landing pattern...but it was an uncomfortable place to be with four huge buzzing propellers behind. He gently banked the plane more to the southeast, crossing over expansive parking, the huge building facility of Santa Rosa Mall, the busy four lanes of Mary Esther Boulevard.

Drifting across the broad scope of Fort Walton Beach High School, he recognized Holy Trinity Lutheran Church, its high peaked roof, the shape of a white dove crowning its height. Across Highway 98, over the International House of Pancakes and the picnic tables of Liza Jackson Park Thorsby banked straight east along the edge of Santa Rosa Sound following the highway which, in a mile or so, would be Fort Walton Beach's Main Street.

At this low altitude Thorsby could clearly define Fort Walton Beach's City Hall with it's unique, round, council chamber, the Boat Marina and it's small ship headquarters nudged close to Saint Simon's-On-The-Sound Episcopal Church, the Chamber of Commerce offices, the long white red-lettered sign of Wayne Patton Realty. These were all places with which Thorsby was intensely familiar...over decades of years. For a few seconds, watching them from the air, he almost forgot the jet fighter which was seeking them.

Nearing the graceful arch of Brooks Bridge he banked south across Santa Rosa Sound toward the ocean...the Gulf of Mexico. Over the big circular tank of the Gulfarium he veered sharply east along the beach, smiling wryly as he glanced quickly at a show in progress with tourists lining the rim of the big tank and Dolphin diving, twisting, leaping to snag a fish from the mouth of a showman. Close beside the Gulfarium..., then quickly behind..., was Wayside Park and the long slender finger of the Okaloosa Island Pier jutting far out into the ocean. Beyond that a brief row of motels and low condos drifted past under them, then four miles or so of open Air Force beach barren except for a couple of round-domed radar sites, an elegant beach club for officers, one a bit less classy for non-commissioned.

In mere seconds, below their wings, was the blue-emerald water of Destin's East Pass... it's narrow channel connecting the thirty mile expanse of Choctawhatchee Bay with ocean waters.

There was only a moment to glance left out of the plastic bubble of the P-51's cockpit canopy to snug, yacht-busy, Destin Harbor as Thorsby heard the roar and whine close behind them and the sleek, gleaming form of the F-16 slid past on their right side. Thorsby chuckled. His judgement had been right on target. The F-16 could not hold the P-51's slow speed...sliding on past, moving at least 40 miles per hour faster. The pilot, staring intensely, looked them over thoroughly, then circled, slipped slowly past them again.

A bare fifty feet separated their wingtips. The jet was in nose-high attitude, razor sharp wings clawing to stay in the air, landing flaps drooping at the back edge of the wing, leading edge slats angled down on the front, landing gear down, virtually hanging in the air on the thunder of the jet engine that overwhelmed sounds in their own cockpit. It was obvious the pilot was doing everything possible to slow enough to look them over. Thorsby grinned again...more broadly this time.

The voice of the jet's pilot crackled into their earphones, "Eglin, this is Red Leader. I don't know what the hell it is. This guy looks like one of those old World War II class B movies. It's some old geezer with a gray moustache. He's got earphones crushed down over an officer's hat. Not even wearing a flight helmet. Doesn't look like he could hurt anybody. It's some kind of antique prop job. Looks like one of those puddle jumper fighter-types from about a half century ago."

"Well, Red Leader, the target crew says somebody blew up the truck next to your target," The voice of Eglin Control had a sarcastic edge. "You see anybody else around?"

"That jerk!" Anger razored an edge to the Angel's voice as sharp as the jet's wings. "We don't have to sit around here, listen to these insults. We've got places to go and people to see. Pour the coal to it, pal."

"Full throttle?" The P-51 surged ahead as he smoothly slid the throttle bar forward, the blurred arc of the huge prop rapidly building speed, finally pulling away from the sleek jet hanging at near stall.

"All the way to the firewall, pal."

"Wait a minute, Eglin," the voice of the jet's pilot crackled again in the earphones, "he's trying to get away. You want me to shoot him down?"

"If it's an antique like you say," the voice of Eglin Control drawled back , "I doubt he can outrun you, Red Leader. He's one of ours isn't he? Why don't you just stay with him a couple of minutes, see what he does? Give us a minute-by-minute."

"Roger, Eglin. Clean again, flaps and gear up. Had to go into afterburner for a couple of seconds, coming up on him again."

At the controls of the P-51, with the Angel leaning forward behind him, Thorsby felt a sense of elation, excitement as the throbbing power of the engine grew, speed built swiftly. The beaches 800 feet below streaked under them faster, faster. Beach houses, row upon row of sky high condominiums, colorful Hobie catamarans, white crests of waves breaking into shallow emerald green ocean along on the beach flashed past the edge of their wings. As speed passed 400 miles per hour he uneasily put the P-51 into a gentle climb to separate their blazing rush from the hardness of the earth.

Glancing toward the thundering jet fighter racing side by side with them, he gave it's pilot his very best catch-me-if-you-can grin...and a salute.

"Man," the jet pilot's voice crackled over the airwaves, "that old clunker gains speed faster than I thought, we're coming past 450...500...550."

"Wait a minute! Something's not right, Eglin! We're coming up on 600. I never dreamed that old prop job could go that fast." Static crackled in their earphones for a long moment as the voice fell mute.

"Uh-oh!" It was more a gasp than mere words. "He's ...he's going into a cloud!...getting hazy!" Startled now. "He...he seems to be...be dis...disappearing...!" The jet pilot's voice was gritty, confused. "What the hell? I...I can't believe it! He's...he's gone!" Quiet for a lingering moment. "I...I can't...uuhh... see him anymore!"

"Red Leader, uuumm...there are no clouds. Weather report says the sky is perfectly clear."

"No! No,,,, it...it wasn't exactly a cloud. More like a...a fog."

"Red Leader, the temperature's ninety degrees. There shouldn't be a shred of fog, anywhere."

"No, no, not exactly a fog either, Eglin Control ...more like...like a mist. He didn't really fly into it. It just seemed to ...to...like...uh...form around the plane. Just got hazier and hazier around him..., then he disappeared into it. My onboard radar doesn't show him anymore. Eglin, are you showing him on radar?"

"Hold a minute, Red Leader. Mmmmm...No... that's a negative! We're not showing him on radar either. Can you go back and check the mist or fog or cloud or whatever it is again?"

"Eglin, I'm circling the spot, now. Uhhh...the mist seems to be gone."

"Red Leader..." silence, puzzlement hung suspended in the radio waves, "...you say a cloud formed around the plane? He disappeared into it? He didn't come out of it? And now the plane and the cloud are both gone?" The quiet hung again.... long this time. "Do we read you right?"

"Uhhh, at the moment that seems to be what ...uhhh... what happened," the pilot of the jet fighter sounded bewildered, far from sure. "Unless, of course, you have...uhhh... other information?"

"Red Leader, we still don't show him anywhere on radar."

"Yeah...and there's no sign here on the ground, or in the water, of a crash."

"You mean...like... he just disappeared in mid-air, Red Leader?"

"Eglin, I'm getting low on fuel," the jet pilot's voice seemed weary.

"Roger, Red Leader, you're cleared to return to base. We'll need a debriefing when you get back to the operations building."

Chapter Eight

Aboard the hurtling P-51 vision was obscured by mist surrounding them. Flying blind, without instrument training, Thorsby fought to hold the plane on an even keel...,guiding, as best he could, by the artificial horizon on the instrument panel. The white cloud-like vapor streamed around them like steam blasting from a release valve ...indicating fearful speed he could never have imagined, speed that seemed to be actually..., fearfully..., increasing.

"Throttle back to 265, easy cruise," the Angel leaned forward behind him again. "I'll put 'er on automatic pilot."

"We...we seem to be going so...so much faster than that," his voice was taut with misgiving of speed so immense that light reflecting through cloud-like variations in density of the haze around them flickered like lightning.

"We're in our envelope of air, but carried in an outer stream moving at a rate hard to describe in human terms," the Angel's voice was relaxed.

"Are we going to....to...?" his voice faltered, unable to speak the word.

"Almost. Not quite...," the Angel chuckled. "If we go all the way there, you can't come back, pal. My guess is, you've got lots left to do over here."

"Oh." There was a flood of relief, comfort, in that. He thought about it for the span of a dozen slow breaths. "Then," he asked, "why are we going."

"Straighten me out if I'm wrong here, pal," the Angel's voice was knowing. "If I understand the reason they gave me for this trip, you've had a nasty surprise, a real knocker of a life-change, the kind of unfairness a lot of guys don't make it past at your age."

In stunning surprises, excitement, he'd forgotten the overwhelming sense of loss, the deep fear that life as it had been, as he willed it to continue, was drawing toward a thing without meaning or purpose, sunk in despair, hopelessness. "How did you know?" he asked of the Angel.

The Angel's knowing chuckle was a comforting sound. "Why do you think they sent me?" he asked in return. "Ya' know, pal, sometimes people are given the chance to hear it straight from the horse's mouth, from those who've been there be-fore, who've fought the good fight, made it, in one way or another."

This time it was long before he answered. "Why me?" he finally broke the dangling silence. "Sure...,the pope, a bishop, maybe a pastor, someone who's lived perfectly on the right track." His head denied it, a slow no-no shake. "Me....? I've made enough mistakes in my time..." his words trailed into silence again, inadequate to express the depth of it.

He'd grown accustomed to the Angel's infec-tious laughter, but it came suddenly, heartily. "Haven't we all, pal?" the tone was just as light, cheering. "Welcome to the human race. If there's a thing perfect about us, it's our constant imper-fection. Main thing is to rely on Him...not on our-selves so much. Maybe you've done better with that than you think."

He grew silent again, wondering about it.

"I guess," the Angel persisted, "you think once we're on the other side we understand everything perfectly. Look at the mistake I made in misjudg-ing that target. Got carried away with the chance to do it again. Just didn't stop to think."

"That could happen to anyone."

"Of course, there's the other thing...," the Angel's tone was confiding, words touched with lingering regret. "The mistake I made that night in July 1949. I was selfish to love flying, to go on doing it... 'til it hurt people dear to me."

"Are you sure it was your fault?"

"I should have handled it..." the Angel words were paced, now, muted, "...somehow." He seemed to be foraging for the right words. "The worst, old buddy, is the sense of failure. Like every fighter pilot, I thought I was the best in the world. Then, suddenly, in the most awful way, I wasn't good enough." He was silent for a moment, one that stretched, lengthened. "So, it's back to old Auxiliary Field #1. Fly the pattern again and again. Work to get it right."

He did not speak for a long time, comparing in his mind the Angel's words to his own sense of failure and defeat at the inconceivable, the unexpected.

Chapter Nine

It was a sense of slowing in the streaking rush of vapor around them, a change in the texture of the tunnel of cloud, a gradual thinning, lightening of opacity, that shook him out of his musing. Bit's of blue sky and glimmers of sunshine began to flicker through the haze. The P-51 began to feel the air around it again, subtle bumping, shying movements over atmospheric ruts and potholes. The mist faded, dissolved at a quickening pace like steam in cool air. The plane blew free of haze into a panorama of rich pastel hues. Below them was soft leafy green, the rich blue of water, a sense of peace and beauty hard to imagine. Above, in the pale azure of sky, an armada of small white fleecy clouds sailed rank upon rank, a few hundred feet above the cockpit canopy of the fighter plane, drifting upriver from a sea.

"Okay, pal, the autopilots off. She all your's again."

The clear plastic bubble which shields the P-51's pilot from the wind stream gives an unhindered 360 degree view around the plane, but there was little time to look at the startling change from streaming, cloying white mist to the beauty and color surrounding him. The plane was already down to a thousand feet on final approach to a runway barely three miles dead ahead. Hurriedly, smoothly he throttled down to final approach speed, moved the mixture control to full rich, pressed carburetor heat on, lowered landing gear and wing flaps, cranked the canopy open. In the busy seconds it took for the runway to race near he had time only to glance across the mile wide expanse of ocean-blue river which paralleled their flight path, to glimpse on the opposite shore an immense, resplendent city sprawled over hills and flat-lands along the river, stretching miles to the sea.

His attention had to be riveted on the runway rushing up to meet their path of flight. It seemed a long, narrow concrete magnet drawing the P-51 from the sky, expanding rapidly in the three panels of his windscreen as the plane approached. The runway looked a couple of thousand feet shorter than Auxiliary Field #1. He gauged the downward slope of flight to touch just beyond the runway's edge. The fighter slowed more than he thought, sinking toward grass short of the concrete. He pushed the throttle bar forward, added a burst of power to float, to stretch the glide. When he knew it was within reach he throttled back, idling the twelve cylinders. The staccato, clattering backfire of the engine reverberated in the wind flutter around the open cockpit.

"Wheeeew!," the Angel whistled over his shoulder as the two main wheels of the landing gear greased onto the concrete a bare hundred feet past the runway's beginning. The plane was instantly, solidly on the ground rolling firmly, swiftly down the length of the runway. "Way to go, pal, a landing doesn't get any better than that one."

He could have braked the fighter to a stop halfway, but he let it roll fleetly the last 1500 feet to the runway's end, tail wheel gently settling to the ground behind him. He turned off onto a hard grassy parking area, locked the left toe brake and revved the engine in a blast of power that spun the plane smartly around until the prop was pointing again toward the runway. As it stopped moving, he flipped the master switch that shut the big Rolls Royce Merlin down. The eleven foot arc of the prop wind-milled lazily, slower, stopped, lurched backward a quarter turn, was still. He sat hunched toward the instrument panel a few moments, checking instruments with the Angel, flipping the switches necessary to finish the shutdown procedure.

Chapter Ten

As THEY CLIMBED OUT of the plane onto the wing he tossed the hat and earphones back into the seat, dropped the parachute on the metal surface. Following the Angel he hopped to the ground from the backside of the wing. They walked around the wing and stood near the big prop stretching, flexing arms and legs to loosen muscles taut from intensity, time spent in the cramped cockpit. Super-heated air wavered around the hot exhaust stacks on the sides of the engine nacelle. Small ticking sounds of hot, cooling, metal resonated from the big engine. He should, he thought, have been exhausted from the energy expended in an unfamiliar, fast moving environment. Instead, to his wonder, he felt refreshed, rested, strong, vibrantly alive, serene, sure of his being.

"Doesn't look like rain, pal," the Angel glanced up at the puffy cotton-ball clouds drifting overhead. "I think we can leave the canopy open and the parachute there on the wing."

"No, rain doesn't seem likely," his glance crossed a graceful span of sky and clouds and trees, a great expanse of farm fields around the airfield. Three dozen or so airplanes were parked in a row next to the P-51. Beyond the landing strip, the green grass of it's shoreline, was the deep blue of the river, far across, the city beyond. The scent of flowers reminded him of Florida in Spring when millions of orange trees along miles of highway are in full bloom, and the fragrance of orange blossom is everywhere, pervading the air. Here, there was far more than orange blossom. Rose and apple sweetened the air, peach, gardenia, lilac, honey suckle, magnolia, heather, ground flowers, each in it's turn at the caprice of warm docile winds. Amid that bouquet of life and growth, the aura of fresh grass and green leaves and flowering things, was the salty tang of the sea, borne the few miles from the shore. "It's hard to imagine a day more beautiful than this."

"It's not a monotonous thing," the Angel expanded on his thought, "with perfect weather all the time. We have rain and storms just like you. There's hot weather in summer and snow in winter. Something for everybody. There are places we can go where winter lasts much longer; places like the tropics where it's warm year round. And places like Northwest Florida where winter is short, where spring and summer and fall make up most of the year. It's easy to go back and forth between climates when we want a change."

The sun glowed warm on skin, air crisp, cool, dry. The temperature so balmy and mild it was hard to tell where skin stopped and breeze began. He unbuttoned cuffs of the flight-suit, rolled the sleeves, pushed them up to biceps, baring his arms. He un-zipped the flight suit down to his belt buckle, opened three buttons of the brightly striped short sleeve shirt. It wasn't that it was hot. It was just that the breeze, the warmth of the sun, the mildness, the scent of the air felt so good, so exhilarating.

"It's this way," the Angel beckoned him on. They walked around the end of the landing strip past the long row of planes. The planes were of different types and sizes, each looking, as the Angel had said, like a thing very special to someone.

As they walked, waves and greetings were exchanged with a man and a woman at separate aircraft. The man was washing a red bi-wing plane with white stripes angling across the wings. "That guy's got a Pitts Special, a stunt plane," he turned to the Angel. "And that lady's got an old J-3 Piper

Cub." The woman was working with tools inside the engine nacelle of the small, yellow high-wing plane.

"Yeah," the Angel grinned as they walked together, "they're here most every day. Flying means a lot to them, too. I learned to fly in a yellow J-3 Cub just like that one." The runway was set back more than two hundred yards from the river. Short grass, freshly mown, extended on all sides of the small landing strip to the farm fields beyond. The green lawn down to the river was bare of trees, planted with round and square beds of colorful flowers. Along the river, as far as he could see, was a wide stone walkway edged with small shrubbery.

On the side opposite the river, freshly mowed grass ended several hundred yards away at farm fences. In that large green lawn were many small trees, widely spaced, with smooth light gray bark and slender trunks. Though only twenty or thirty feet tall, their foliage was tightly knit, bushy, casting wide circles of shade. In the shade were three small groups of people sitting on the grass with picnic baskets open. He glanced up into the pale blue of the sky, through the ranks of small cottony clouds, "It must be close to noon here," he said.

"Yeah, pal, it's almost lunch time," the Angel said. "I'm hungry again."

They reached the river's edge, turned away from the landing strip, walked along the stone pathway around a grassy mound that had blocked view in that direction.

CHAPTER ELEVEN

BEYOND THE LOW HILL, a hundred feet or so up from the river stood a rectangular open-air forum edged on all sides by white fluted columns spaced a dozen feet apart, stretching twenty feet toward the sky. At the single, wide, stone step leading to the marble floor, he hesitated, awed by the massive size and magnificence of the gathering place.

"There are some people I want you to meet," the Angel smiled waving him onward. Their shoes tapped, echoed hollowly on gleaming gray marble squares as they paced down the immense length of the forum.

"This thing must be a hundred fifty feet wide and a football field long," he glanced at the Angel walking to his left. Far down, near the end of the forum, was a row of tent-like shelters set side by side, not quite touching. There were five of them, each perhaps twenty-five feet wide, forty feet long. Canvas hued in broad bands of emerald green and white shaded the marble underneath them, tapering down supports at the four corners of each tent. Scalloped roof-edging of the same

85

fabric and color, trimmed with white binding, gave the tents a bazaar-like air, fit, he thought, for a royal wedding.

"Yeah, it's really something isn't it, old buddy?," the Angel said as they continued to move toward a small group of people gathered around a long table under the tent nearest the riverside. "They set up the tents so a lot of people can move around 'em easily. There'll be a big crowd here near suppertime."

The ground at the edge of the forum, which sloped upward to within a few inches of the marble floor, was covered with deep green, luxuriant, carefully manicured lawn. Shrubbery, planted a few feet apart around all four sides of the forum floor, combined the sense of a low green wall with the feeling of freedom and open space. Wide single-step entrances at the center of each side brought a sense of welcome, of easy coming or going. The white fluted pillars, reaching far above his head, marked with might and timeless serenity the boundary of the gathering place, yet left wide open the un-hindered vistas of green grass, shade trees, shrubbery, flowers, river waters, and broad farm fields surrounding it.

As their pace brought them nearer, his eyes were drawn to those under the tent because there was no one else. They stood waiting, expectant, close-knit, near a graceful, massive oak table perhaps a dozen feet long. It was covered with brilliant white linen, elegantly set for dining. As they came closer, he saw there were seven placements at one end, extending near the center. The other half was laden with dishes of steaming food. The warm scent of Sunday dinner, of fresh baked bread, roast turkey, baked ham and hot gravy, steaming vegetables, fresh fruit's, was carried on the breeze from the river toward them while they were yet many steps away.

"Mmmmm," he whispered to the Angel, "smell that food! The peanut butter crackers and Grapette didn't last long, I'm starved again."

"Yeah," a grin lighted the Angel's face as their steps brought them to the edge of the tent, "they really know how to put on the feed bag when company comes."

"Welcome, Jemison Thorsby." It was a small man with flowing white hair and beard who stepped forward, hand outstretched, smile warm with recognition. A white linen robe, gathered at the waist and cinched with a leather strap that matched brown sandals on his feet, flowed loosely around his body.

"Thor," the Angel's arm circled his shoulders,

"this is Job."

"Job...?" The inherent habit of courtesy over-came amazement, let him reach out in reflex motion to clasp the small hand in his larger one. His glance toward the Angel was a startled one. "...from..." he stammered, "...from the Old Testament?" The smile of the white robed man before him broadened into gentle laughter at his surprise.

"Takes some gettin' used to, doesn't it, pal?" the Angel grinned, squeezing his shoulder in the warmth of friendship.

"To say the least...," he struggled with a sense of wonder, much as he had at the Angel's appearance. "But, I'm really glad to meet you." The words seemed clumsy, awkward, hardly enough.

"And this lady," the Angel guided him toward the second introduction, "you'll remember as Grandma Moses."

"We're glad you're here, Mr. Thorsby." The twinkle in her eyes, the strength of her smile, belied a bird-like frailness. Her glasses were small, round, gold rimmed. Her dress dark in color, neatly patterned. Over it she wore a soft button-front sweater. The welcome in her touch was sure, undeniable, as she took both his hands in her own.

"Thank you," his try at a half-bow was courtly, perhaps a bit self-conscious. "Your paintings are beautiful. And the songbook...so many of them are wonderful old favorites." It was hardly adequate to describe the remarkable success of her talent, but he could think of nothing to add as the Angel nudged him toward the next person.

"Thor, this is Plato." The man, too, was less tall than the Angel, robust in stature, dressed in the white toga-like robes of the ancient Roman and Greek era.

"How are you, Sir?" What else, he wondered, could one say to say to a figure so imposing in earthly history.

"Very well, thank you," Plato's demeanor seemed intense, active rather than scholarly. "We thought you'd be here earlier. Something must have interfered with your trip."

"Thor, was flying the Mustang. He's gettin' pretty good at it," the Angel interrupted. "I was the one who miscalculated a bit on the way over."

"Not again!" He wore the stars of a United States Army General. The uniform, jodphur pants and calf length boots, were from the era of the first World War. "What happened this time, Lieutenant?"

"Well, sir, with Thor on board the Mustang,

we had the chance to make a real strafing run." There was more than a hint of embarrassment in the Angel's voice. "There was no way to know the old abandoned truck we fired on would be loaded with explosives."

"Quite the big bang, I assume?" the General's tone was rather dry.

"As a matter of fact, sir, it was a bit of a surprise," the Angel replied. "No real harm done, though. I'll watch for the chance to make amends when they need help."

"See that you do, Lieutenant. Call on me if I can be of assistance."

Finally, a smile brightened the General's face. "So!, this is the man we came to meet. Welcome, Thorsby, I'm Billy Mitchell. I see you're wearing a flight suit. Are you an officer and pilot."

"Far from it, sir. I had several years of reserve officers training and national guard duty. Never the regulars. Rob, lent me the flight suit for the trip over."

"Ah, a citizen soldier! The backbone of our defense," the general nodded appreciatively. "Good man, Thorsby."

"But, to give due credit, sir," the Angel intervened, "Thor, here, has some quite natural skills as a pilot."

"To have skills as a pilot can be as effective at sea as in the air," the fifth member stepped forward from the small group.

"Thor, this is Christopher Columbus." The Angel gestured toward the man dressed in the canvas clothing of a sailor, shirt laced from near waist to neckline.

"Welcome, Thorsby, we've been waiting for you." Columbus stepped forward to grasp his outstretched hand. "You live near the sea, and you are a sailor, too." Columbus eyes were intense, inquisitive, friendly.

"How did you know?" There was a strong sense of intelligence, decisiveness, comradery about the man. Thorsby liked him immediately.

"A sailor has a way about him that other sailors perceive." Columbus leaned forward in a confiding way. "Perhaps it is the same with navigators of the air."

"Maybe so! You're right on target, though. I sailed for many years. My little boat was less than twenty-five feet long, far smaller than the Nina, or the Pinta, or the Santa Maria that brought you to America." How odd it seemed to say those words to the man.

"What was the name of your vessel?" Columbus asked.

91

"Morningstar." It gave him a good feeling just to say it again. Always, there was the rush of happiness, pleasure, remembrance... hundreds of joyous hours spent with his children in the tiny ship.

"They called Jesus himself the Morningstar," Columbus nodded approval. "It's a fine name for a vessel."

"It's half past the noon hour," Job's voice joined them again. "The food is ready. Lets sit down and eat as we visit together. Jemison Thorsby, you are the guest of honor. Your place is at the head of the table."

He opened his mouth to demur, pressed by the feeling that one of these towering figures of history merited that seat. Before he could speak, the Angel, hand on his shoulder, guided him to the chair. He stood until the Angel seated Grandma Moses and the others chose seats. Looking down the length of the table, his view swept over the serenity of the flowered lawn, the deep blue of water, the mile-wide expanse of river, the mammoth, sparkling city beyond.

"Rob," Job looked across the table to the Angel.

"It's your turn."

Heads bowed, quiet, expectant. Suddenly, in his mind's eye, Thorsby could see the family gatherings of childhood. The farm, overlooking backwaters of Chesapeake Bay, was their grandparents summer home. Often in summer, sometimes at Christmas, they were all there together...his parents, four aunts, three uncles, eight cousins, grandparents. He felt again the press of warmth and closeness around the long table on the screened sun porch, gentle laughter, the reserved, courtly conversation of old Virginia families. Was it only coincidence that the Angel's words of grace were words he treasured, words his grandfather had spoken at so many family gatherings.

"Father, make us truly thankful for these and all our blessings."

Bowls of steaming food were lifted from the table's end, passed from hand to hand. Plates of delicate bone china, trimmed with double rings that matched the gleaming gold of knives and forks and spoons, waited to receive the bounty. Large stemmed crystal goblets stood brimming with sweetened ice tea chilled by chips of ice. Smaller ones held dark red wine with the hearty, peppery tang of Beaujolais or Sauvignon. He bit into a hot, buttered roll. It's crusty, yeasty, mouth-watering flavor sent hunger soaring. Edges of roast turkey slices were brown, crisp, the meat itself light, delicious, moist, tender. Ham, seasoned with spikes of cloves, was baked to a golden turn. There was gravy to flood mashed potatoes; succotash, the spring-fresh corn and tender green lima mélange that livens early summer tables in the deep South; sliced tomatoes, deep red, juicy; golden squash sauteed with onions; broad pods of country pole beans long simmered with pork; cool sliced cucumbers in vinegar; verdant broad leaves of collard greens stewed to languorous softness; bronze tender field peas, the omnipotent staple of the Southern household, boiled with bit's of carved ham to rich, brothy tenderness. Could it be, he marveled, that the whole world and Heaven, too, acknowledged the wonder of Southern food?

Moments of quiet were transgressed by the gentile clink of golden eating utensils against china plates, the ring of crystal goblets, murmurs of shared appreciation. In those muted mentions he grasped that the fare of his region of America had been unknown to them, though they seemed beguiled by it's Southern succulence. It was clear that the bountiful table had been prepared especially for his visit. That realization gave Jemison Thorsby quite a bit more on which to reflect.

"You're familiar with my paintings?" Grandma Moses words bore an aura of contentment, a sense that laughter was always just a glance away. In her face he could feel the quiet firmness, the sureness, the strength of purpose about her.

"So many of us, all over the world, love your paintings," he said. "I've seen them many times in magazines and newspapers. A lot of art museums have them on display. They call your work the last genuine expression of American folk art, the art of the pioneers."

"Yes," a smile lighted Grandma Moses face, "I was so surprised, at first, when Mr. Kallir, Otto Kallir, began to sponsor my paintings at the Galerie St. Etienne in New York. And after that beginning, there were so many exhibitions there. It was like a dream come true."

"It's incredible that you started painting when you were 78," he replied, "and painted with such success for more than twenty years."

"It was something I'd always wanted to do," Grandma Moses looked directly into his eyes and the words came on wings of laughter, "a thing I dearly loved. Age itself should never keep us from learning, from trying new things. It should never stop us from finding a new path, from doing the things we really want to do."

"So, Jemison Thorsby, you already know of Grandma Moses," they all turned to Job as he spoke. "Do you know of me?"

He chewed a mouthful of bread, washed it down with sweet tea, gathering the scattered memories of Sunday school lessons before answering.

"We still have a saying over there...'the patience of Job'." He spoke uncertainly, at first, then more surely as recollections grew. "Of all the men of the Old Testament, you had the most enduring faith."

"Can you imagine?" Job's words were intense, measured. "In the face of all that was taken from me, how hard that might seem?"

"Well...lets see," he crossed his fingers under the table, hoping the numbers were somewhere near correct. "God allowed Satan to take away your seven sons and three daughters, along with thousands of sheep and camels and cattle. Oh, and a lot of donkeys, too. Then you lost all your wealth, and all your servants except for three. And then, your body became covered with painful sores."

"When God sends us good things," Job's finger, tapping the linen tablecloth, underscored his meaning, "we welcome them. Why should we complain when he sends us trouble?"

"Your trouble was so...," he groped for the right word, couldn't find one that truly described it, "...so terrible!"

"Indeed, it was a most painful time," Job agreed.

"If I remember right," Thorsby said it musingly, struggling to recall the end of the Book, "in keeping faith you were given back double what was taken from you."

"You know it well," Job laughed. "There were fourteen thousand sheep, and six thousand camels, two thousand head of cattle, and a thousand donkeys. And then there were seven sons and three daughters. And a hundred and forty more years to enjoy prosperity, grandchildren, great grandchildren."

"The thing to wonder is...," Thorsby felt troublesome saying it, "...how many of us average folks can hold on when things seem so hopeless?"

"Life gives us moments," Job said, "when all we have left is faith, along with the values and talents which built our lives."

97

"I'm finding that out, it seems."

"The real risk," Job leaned forward in his seat, "is to abandon them in a passing season of despair. Then we could lose far more than possessions or wealth. We could lose ourselves."

"Well said, my friend," there was an aura of self assurance, of quiet forcefulness in the sailor's voice. "Press on in faith...and often you'll do far more than you planned."

Thorsby chuckled, shifted self consciously in his chair, as Columbus eyes turned to him. "You mean, like sailing toward India and finding an entire new continent?"

"Ah, you know of my misadventures, too?" Columbus' intense interest in the conversation showed in the gleam of brown eyes, his engaging smile.

"If I remember classroom history," he gestured back toward the sailor, "it took six years before you could persuade King Ferdinand and Queen Isabella of Spain to back your venture."

"There, you see?" Columbus gestured with both hands. "Faith!..in your ideas!...in yourself! Keep trying...and one day you're sailing west, headed for Japan, with the sure feeling that you are on a new, shorter trade route to India."

"American histories of your first voyage in

1492 say your crew grew rebellious," said Thorsby, "afraid you were going to sail off the edge of a flat earth."

"Not true," Columbus shook his head. Most seafarers and learned people of that time knew the earth was round."

"How," muttered Thorsby, "can text books be so mistaken?"

"To be honest," Columbus added "we did have some difficulty raising a crew. Many sailors feared, in such a long voyage, we might not find land soon enough to keep from starving. It took many weeks to raise the crew of 90, but by far, they were trained, highly experienced seamen. Except for three, of course, that came from local jails. Besides, they were very well paid. Ship masters and pilots made 2,000 maravedis a month. Sailors made 1,000, and apprentices made 666 maravedis a month."

"Well whaddya know ?" Thorsby interjected. "I've never seen mention of your sailors pay."

"The voyage went rather smoothly," Columbus continued. "We were sailing downwind, to the southwest, on trade winds that blow steadily from the northeast in those latitudes. We had good winds and not much complaint from the crew. It was at 2:00 a.m. on October 12, 1492 that Juan Barmejo on the Pinta spotted a light. After dawn we anchored at an island the Indians called Guanahani. We renamed it San Salvador."

"Such an amazing thing," Thorsby leaned back in his chair. "You start out on a voyage headed for India, and end up discovering a whole new world."

"Well," it was Plato who entered the conversation, "it may have been a new world to Europeans, but it was a very old world, and home, to thousands of people who lived there."

"So very true," Columbus glanced toward Plato, then back toward Thorsby. "In all four voyages, I never realized I was not in, or near, Asia. I made two miscalculations. First I thought the Asian continent stretched 30 degrees farther east than it actually does. I correctly used the 360 degree division of the globe, but was wrong in my estimate of the length of a degree at the earth's equator. Those miscalculations misled me to think Japan was 2,760 miles from the Canary Islands. Actually it is 12,190 miles. And, of course, like other Europeans then, I had no idea that two massive continents lay in the ocean between."

"Faith is like that," Plato spoke again. "It often leads us in better, unexpected, paths."

"There's nothing like sticking to your guns,"

General Mitchell added to the thought.

"Thorsby," Plato's smile was open, friendly, "are you familiar with my writings?"

"Only in the broadest sense." He leaned back in his chair, a distant look in his eyes as he struggled once again to recall school classes. "You took the ideas of Socrates, added your own thoughts, then through your own writings and the writings of your student Aristotle, passed these ideas down to the Roman and modern worlds."

"That's a very simple analysis of it," Plato shrugged.

"Well, to put it more clearly," Thorsby went on, "the dialogues of Socrates which you wrote became the starting point for most of the ideas and philosophy of the modern world."

"It is still a rather broad outline," a hint of smile returned to Plato's face.

"You left your home in Athens and stayed away for ten years," Thorsby said, old school lessons beginning to creep back more surely from memory. "You were discouraged by the viciousness of politics after the long war between Athens and Sparta."

"Yes! The Peloponnesian war," Plato interjected. "It began in 431 B.C. and lasted 27 years."

"I was never good at remembering history

dates," Thorsby conceded. "Well, anyway, you wrote that the problems of the human race will never disappear until those who have political power also have God's gift of true wisdom and philosophy."

"That's more like it," Plato's smile widened.

"Your idea, then," Thorsby added, "was to go home to Athens and start an Academy, the first European university. You wanted to teach the young to love wisdom, truth, and justice. You hoped to bring about political reform through education and persuasion. Your Academy lasted for something like 900 years.

"Aha! Now you've got it!" Plato clapped his hands together, half rising from his chair. "It lasted until the time of the Roman emperor Justinian. He closed the Academy in 529 A.D. Socrates believed that virtue was a form of knowledge that could be taught. I believed more should be added to prepare men to be leaders. I included studies in mathematics, astronomy, music, and logic, as well as politics and ethics. The truth is, only by strict discipline can young minds be made keen enough to look beyond the disorder of politics and see the unchangeable principals of truth."

"I hate to be the bearer of bad news," Thorsby shook his head in mock disgust. "The world's political mess isn't much better than you found it in your time."

"Hey, pal, what are you, some kind of professor?" it was the Angel, laughing, who gestured toward him from across the table. Everyone joined in the laughter, Plato the heartiest.

"Hardly," he was glad to feel a part of the merriment. "I do read a lot, though. Learn a world of interesting things that way. For instance, Plato was the first to say seriously that women should be equals with men in public life. He was first to set fundamental rules of logical reasoning. His pupil, Aristotle, made logic into a science."

"Plato's 'Dialogues'," Thorsby took a deep breath and continued, "showed us the way in politics and economics, sociology and ethics." He paused, frowning with the effort to remember. "His influence is still felt in modern times in city planning, health regulation, business, government administration. Even Alexander the Great used Plato's ideas as models for legislation in Greece and Asia and Egypt after they were conquered by his father, Philip of Macedonia. After that, the Romans used parts of those laws for their imperial codes, so Plato is often called the father of European jurisprudence."

"Good grief," the Angel gave him a look of pretended dismay. "You have been reading a lot!"

"What's more," Thorsby went on, "the Romans used a modified version of Plato's program of education and passed it on to the Middle Ages, beyond that to the Renaissance."

"Don't forget," Plato said, "it all came about after what seemed to us the end of everything...the accusations against Socrates, his trial, his death sentence."

In the midst of their sharing Thorsby found a quiet, unspoken, gnawing certainty that flourished as they measured the learning, the experiences of their lives. In his heart he was sure that he was not yet a part of that splendid, peaceful place. Instead was a growing eagerness to be on his way, to be in the busy cockpit of the P-51, headed to small towns and the sea. Home to a place where life, even in random failure and defeat, challenges the defiant spirit. Home to a place where peace and certainty are not yet fully born, but hoped for, searched for, gathered a little each day with effort, and fear, and strife.

"That seems," General Billy Mitchell touched Grandma Moses shoulder in silent apology for speaking across her, "to be a recurring pattern among us. Thorsby, are you familiar with my military career?"

"Aviation has become such a big thing in our world," Thorsby spread his hands to express the magnitude of it, "sure, I've read about it. You were a part of aviation leadership from the time the army bought it's first plane from the Wright brothers. You paid for your own flying lessons and pushed hard for greater use of the airplane in the army."

"Good man! You're right on target so far." The General looked pleased.

"You were a leader in air operations in the first World War," Thorsby recounted, "and flew your own plane a great deal over enemy territory."

"Right again," Mitchell smiled.

"After the war you were made assistant chief of the Army Air Services, but you knew War Department officials did not understand the need for air power. They repeatedly rejected your efforts to expand military aviation. So, you went straight to the American public with books and articles."

"Government officials don't like that! I knew someone had to do it! Aviation was going to be needed in the next war." The General banged his fist on the table.

"In 1921 you told them bombers could sink their supposedly invincible battleships. They didn't believe it, so you proved it by sinking two of them. Then in 1923 you bombed and sank two more."

"That's it," Mitchell grinned, "the captured German Ostfriesland and the old USS Alabama in 1921. Then the old ships New Jersey and Virginia in 1923."

"In Congressional committee hearings, held to analyze the importance of those sinkings, you severely criticized the policies of the War and Navy Departments. They still didn't believe aviation was important. In 1925. To get even with you, they removed you as Assistant Chief of the Army Air Service, and demoted you from General to Colonel."

"It was a humiliating day, even though I knew I was right," the General shook his head.

"Then, the Navy dirigible Shenandoah crashed with heavy loss of life. You made public charges against government officials."

"Dead right! Somebody needed to do it," anger swept the General's face. "I charged them with incompetency, criminal negligence, and almost treasonable administration of national defense."

"So," Thorsby continued, "they court martialed you, found you guilty of insubordination, and suspended you from duty for five years. In early 1926 you resigned your commission in disgust."

"Many of us, over centuries," Mitchell looked defiantly resigned, "have paid a terrible price for intelligence, for knowing our jobs, for trying to look ahead."

"Just 13 years later," Thorsby pieced it all together, "in 1939, Hitler's military forces defeated most of Europe using air power as the main thrust of attack. Isn't it appalling that government officials can be so dreadfully wrong."

"And," added Plato, "so willing to destroy a man's career while they're being dreadfully wrong. It's the same thing that happened to Socrates hundreds of years before."

"Thor," the Angel sensed a peak in the conversation, pushed back his chair, rose to his feet. Everyone had finished eating long before. "I guess we should be heading back," he interjected. "It's getting near mid-afternoon."

"The time has gone so quickly," Thorsby lamented, pushing back his chair. His face betrayed a sense that the exchange was not complete.

"Thorsby," it was Columbus who asked. "Is there something more?"

"I guess...," in a way, it seemed ungrateful to ask, "...I thought you'd give me the big secret to resolving worldly problems. Rob sort of hinted at that on the way over."

The hosts and the Angel glanced silently around at each other as if to choose the one who would answer.

"Truth is, Thorsby," General Mitchell was the one who spoke. "We've shared that in several ways."

"In being here," Columbus added, "we hope we've shown you how important every person is, how important you are, in the scheme of things."

"Faith...," Job stepped toward him, "...the determination to hold on to it, no matter what, makes the difference in the end."

"Lives are different," Grandma Moses moved to him and took both of his hands in her own. "But all our experiences have a common thread. When you've had time to think over the things we've talked about, you'll find you have the answer."

"More to the point," Plato waved his hand, a gesture that encompassed them all, "it will be your answer, one that suit's your needs and talents, one so interesting and fulfilling it won't matter whether it's rewarded by others."

"Thorsby," General Mitchell turned to him again, "has the Lieutenant mentioned there is someone waiting on the pier to see you?"

"At his wish," the Angel jerked a thumb toward the river's edge, "I was saving that for last."

"Waiting to see me?" Thorsby turned to look more intently, his features growing tense at a far distant hint of recognition.

"Yes, he's here with us often," it was Columbus who spoke. "He felt it would be easier if he waited to see you alone."

"I'll wait over by the P-51," the Angel's thumb jerked again, this time toward the low hill and the small airstrip beyond.

Thorsby looked toward each of them once more, a lingering moment, probing for words grand enough, momentous enough to say thank you for the time, the personal attention each of them had given him. In the end, they were the only words that seemed fitting...and he was granted the grace to know they understood.

CHAPTER TWELVE

AT THE EDGE OF THE MARBLE floor, past tall columns and shrubs, a stone path crossed the grassy lawn to the river walkway. Just beyond was the pier, it's wooden deck a step up from the grass, a catfish jump above blue-green, wind rippled water. It was, perhaps, a dozen feet wide, fifty feet long.

The form and posture and bearing of those dear is as familiar as a face. The sureness of who he was came while he was yet a hundred feet away. The clothes, too, marked him. He'd been a professional man in working years, with suit and tie and jeweled stickpin. There'd always been a fine gold railroad watch in one vest pocket, a small gold folding knife in a second, a bright gold chain connecting the two in a gleaming loop from pocket to pocket.

In retirement years, for a reason Thorsby never understood, he'd dressed like a day worker in khaki pants, shirts of rustic plaid. In the unswerving nonconformity of an engineer - comfort and common sense before fashion - he chose the oddness of a straw, African, safari helmet in heat of the sun.

As Thorsby's steps thumped hollowly on planks of the deck, he felt the swelling of inner defense, the familiar tingle of tension, anxiety. It was a matter their discourse had borne for more than half a century. Their's had not been an easy connection, scarcely a thing you could call an alliance, although he was of his blood and, in some ways, of his habit.

Fishing had never been a pastime for them. Oh, a time or two they'd cast lines together from the "Ida Mae" a sturdy, graceful oysterman's rowboat from the Tidewater of the Chesapeake Bay far up in Virginia's northern neck. Thorsby's grandmother had bought the little boat. It was her name it carried.

It was so like him not to turn immediately, to remain intent on the task, hands working, reeling in something that bent the fishing rod in a deep arc toward the water. How long had it been - seven years?...eight? - since he'd seen those hands lying crossed in unending stillness? How many years before had he watched them work with board and pencil, shovel, rake, axe, wrench...ever with care, determination, precision. Gripping a steering wheel, plying tools under the car's hood, guiding wood into a screeching saw blade, how supple, how sure they'd always seemed. The sense of wonder billowed to see once more the strength of fingers, prominent veins, tufts of dark hair, the small brown spots, neatly trimmed nails that were the familiarity of life itself. Oddly, at that moment, he remembered them from the height of a child, hands far closer to small, curious, impressionable eyes than the expressions far above.

At the same time, movement on the bench next to a tackle box drew his eyes. A small black and white head bolted to attention, dark eyes riveted with recognition. In a flash, the small dog, more black than white, had pattered swiftly across the deck to stand on tip-toe, pawing, reaching up to him. Jemison Thorsby backed a step or two to the facing bench, sat down on it's curved wooden slats. In a leap the tiny companion was in his lap, tongue searching his cheeks, eyes seeming to laugh, gleaming with gladness. Far from the waddling, 30 pound, painfully over-weight little friend he'd known...was the trim, lean, sleek, vigorous 7 pounds or so that was good, right for her diminutive size. Satisfied, at last, that it was he, she settled happily into his lap, eyes again adoring the fisherman. The taut fish line surged. There was a sudden upward whip of the pole, the roil of water as the weight of the fish lunged free. In his mind he parried, stiffened, braced himself for the flare of anger, the surly word, the explosive impatience. None came. The hands worked quietly, reeling in wet line, empty hook, placed the rod and reel just-so against the wood rail. Finally the man turned to look fully into his face.

From long uncertain years, Thorsby was braced to see tensely drawn taut-lipped features, the gleam of suspicion and hostility in dark eyes, the defensive stance, to wonder whether anger or indifference would surge forth.

None was there! None! All of it, every bit of it, transfigured. The world around seemed to draw far away as he strained to understand, to take it in. How splendid it was, how different, to see the openness and warmth in those eyes, the trust and kindness and concern in his face, to sense the reaching out, the personal interest in himself, his being. And, like the pilot, to see a startling transformation back to the vigor of mid-life, an appearance Thorsby could so clearly remember from early childhood years.

Even then, he was far from prepared for the

question his father gently asked, "Are you still mad at me?"

In all of their years, far more than a half-century of them, his father had seemed little bothered by what Thorsby might think or feel.

"No...," he lingered over the words wondering if he might choose the wrong ones yet again.

"Not in thirty years," he finally just put it plainly. "I guess, I finally grew up enough to respect your views, even when they didn't make much sense to me."

"My outlook on things, sometimes...maybe too often..., wasn't as considerate of others as it might have been, you know," his father smiled, hands apart in a gesture of contrition as he sat down on the facing bench next to the tackle box.

"It did seem like everything had to be done your way," Thorsby's words were tentative, near a query, paced by the familiar sting of anxiety at the very idea of criticizing. "At the same time," he looked full into his father's face, "I was sure there was no one smarter than you."

"Oh, I was blessed with a good mind," penitence was there to see. "It was the way I looked at things. I never realized until I came here how unbending I'd been." His father's eyes reached far away, beyond the wide river. "It was never easy for me to trust. I could find so many reasons to be angry, resentful. Sometimes, It seemed everybody, everything was out to get me, to make things harder. I see now, how tough I made it...on myself, everyone else."

"So..., Suzie is here with you?" Thorsby fragmented the silence that hung between them.

"Where else would she be?" Long ago, there may well have been haughtiness, biting sarcasm, impatience, in such words. Now, there was none of those things, simply the gentle, quiescent avowal of the way things should be, of the way they were.

"I mean...how did she find you over here...?" The little dog jumped to the deck. In three leaps she was across the space between the two benches, up into his father's lap.

"I dunno...!" He smiled, a hand smoothing her head. Now there was recognizable, classic, himself! If a subject interested him, his attention was intense, focused, moodily pursuing, like a cat creeping up on a mouse. It was far from his way to waste time wondering, worrying about a matter he could do nothing about. "Seems just the natural way of things here. Works out ok...the way it's supposed to, I guess."

"Some people, a lot of 'em, it seems...doubt

that pets come here," Thorsby murmured.

"I appreciate you taking care of what had to be done," his father smiled.

"Its an awful thing to have to do...their little lives near gone...suffering so...!" Thorsby looked at Suzie, strong now, healthy, bright, content.

"But then, in an instant, the sickness, the suffering's over...and she's here, where she needs to be."

"Yes. I see that, now." Thorsby sat on the facing bench, absorbed by serenity as clear as a spring morning, by his father's composure, empathy. Stiff-lipped sternness had become an easy smile, in the eyes a warmth of interest, a give and take he'd never seen before. Whatever had caused the harshness, the anger, the irritability, the criticism...was healed, melted away, reborn.

"Getting canned is no big deal!"

"What?" The abrupt veer of the subject caught Thorsby off guard.

I changed jobs a lot of times."

"Yeah, but near 60, it's no picnic," his was the frown this time. "Finding a new one is not a likely thing."

"Naaaaaa...!!" his father's hand waved the idea away. "I told you a long time ago, it's your business to get ready. Opportunity will come. It'll take care of itself."

"You remember telling me that ?"

"Of course, I remember. It was important, not just some fly-by-night idea. "

"Well, you were right. It's always proved true, 'til now," he nodded in assent. "Maybe it's the age thing that's got me spooked. Anyway, I never got fired before."

"I never waited around. I told 'em what they could do with it!" his father grinned. "Like that song you've got over there now..."You can take this job and shove it...!" In the wink of an eye both were laughing, uproariously, doubled over, gasping for breath.

"Yeah...!" when he could finally catch a breath, "...sometimes I got the idea you looked for a reason to tell 'em to shove it!"

"Well...I loved engineering. I was damned good at it, too." his father's smile was still mischievously wide. "But, to tell the truth I'd rather raise chickens and sell eggs than put up with the dirty buzzards that run the front office." Laughter exploded again.

Now there was another phrase ringing with familiarity, a thing Thorsby could recognize, except for the laughter, the good humor, the sharing. Had it ever been that way before? "I don't think..." he retorted, still trying to catch a breath," ...I don't think you're supposed to say that over here."

"No...No, I suppose not...!" In his lap, jiggled by the force of laughter, Suzie tilted her head far up to look curiously at him. Slowly his features became more composed, serious. "Here's the thing! Age, even some supposed fall from grace ...it's not the end of the world."

"Even though it seems like...?"

"Mull over what our friends up there had to say," his father interrupted, gesturing back toward the huge pavilion. "Before long, you'll see why we asked them to come. Besides, there's plenty of time."

"You know that...?"

"Well, heck now, if you step in front of a bus, fall off a bridge, or you don't take care of your health... then, there's hardly a guarantee...!"

"Yeah...!" Thorsby nodded in agreement. No one could deny the good sense in that.

"Otherwise...there ought to be time to get things going again, time to finish getting ready. Then, plenty of good retirement years, like I had."

"Odd, maybe, I never much wondered about having time. Finding the way to start over has been the bug-a-boo. It's the young guys they want, you know."

"Aren't things changing over there?" Thorsby's father braced a tanned arm against the wood rail, cheek against knuckles, a posture as familiar as the sunrise. "People living longer, healthier, clear minded? ...a lower ratio of young workers?"

"Yeah. The new ones sure make a careless crew," Thorsby nodded. "A lot of them don't care whether they do it right or not."

"Maybe experience is more important than you imagined." Suzie settled down in his lap again. "Anyway, business is the work to be in. There's wide opportunity, not limited to a single purpose. Remember when I said that's what you oughta do?"

"Sure! In the Great Depression engineers were starving, businessmen were wearing diamond rings...?"

"Right! That's exactly what I said...the way it often was, too."

"You were right, then. It's been good to me. Up 'til now, I've done ok....better than ok!"

"A little hard-headed, maybe. A little do-it-your-own-way, maybe...," there was more than a bit of chagrin in his father's wry, self-conscious grin, in the knowing twinkle in his eyes. "I wonder where you might have learned that?"

"I wonder...?" Thorsby rolled his eyes, melodramatically.

As though there was a doubt? Laughter claimed them again. It was hardly a family secret. Thorsby felt his father's gaze upon him.

"You've done it the hard way," his father's eyes held his, unswerving. "But...you're damn good at what you do...!" It wasn't a thing Thorsby had heard often from him.

Silence is a sharing thing when a bond is the way it should be, or, perhaps, at long last so. Moments passed as the two carefully studied the cracks in the deck, the ripples on the deep blue of the river, the armada of fleecy clouds marching toward the sea.

Thorsby, looked toward his father at the sound of his voice.

"It's past mid-afternoon, already." His eyes, narrowed against the sun's glare, appraised it's declining height. "You need to be headed home." He stood and set the tiny black and white dog afoot on the slats of the bench.

"Right," Thorsby agreed, rising to his feet. "Rob's waited at the plane all this time."

"Here." His father stepped to him. The arms

120

around him, his in return, were strong, hearty, equally unforeseen, ...a healing link to years parched for such.

"Don't take any wooden nickels!" It struck him as the core of life, a thing near a light-hearted family liturgy, parting words he'd known all his years. They came from before his time, the era of his father's youth. He'd never fully understood their meaning, but in the desk drawer, in the earliest years he could remember, there had been thin squares of Balsa wood, the words "Wooden Nickel" printed on them.

"I'll be watching for 'em." It was family repartee spoken so often, over so many years.

Thorsby was a hundred feet away before he could turn, look back. The tiny dog was held again, curled on one arm, paws dangling over a hand, looking intently after him. His father waved, hand moving in the terse, brisk, side-to-side gyration that was so familiar. As he rounded the low hill that would bear him out of sight, he glanced back again. Their eyes, another wave, still followed him.

CHAPTER THIRTEEN

"HOW'D IT GO, OLD BUDDY. Ya doin' ok?" the Angel's voice came from behind as he slid into the seat of the P-51 again. Thorsby's fingers were already flipping switches that would breathe life into the plane.

"It's been quite a day...!" He sighed as the big engine caught, thundered into shuddering energy, "...Quite a day...to say the least!"

"Yeah, pal," there was comfort in the Angel's friendly rap on his shoulder, "there's a lot to deal with, the first day over here!"

There was no need for the two young sergeants with their big fire extinguisher to leave, to vanish after the engine started safely, without the danger of fire. They were already home.

In one sense - in the surreal human convergence of us that sorts out feelings, the bond with others, the wracking curiosities of human existence - Thorsby felt wrung out, the hint of it unmistakable in his voice. At the same time was a powerful sense of rejuvenation, of physical energy, of vibrancy, eagerness to be headed back. He couldn't know, in the fullness of the moment, that his inexplicable day was far from over.

Thorsby was glad of the noise, the grumbling clamor of the engine, the clatter of the big prop against air, the buzzing vibration of power in the plane's metal as he let the engine warm up. How good it was, for a while at least, to have other things, demanding things, to think about.

When the oil temperature indicator needled into green, he palmed the throttle bar forward, urging the growl of the engine, the whirling of the big prop to draw the plane to the very end of the runway. A touch of toe onto the left brake, a blast from the big prop spun it around, aiming the long, high-set engine nacelle down the center of the airstrip. Thorsby reached for the round, black, wooden handle and cranked the clear bubble of the canopy closed over, around them. He glanced again at temperature and oil pressure gauges to be sure the twelve cylinders were running properly, safely, then eased the throttle bar forward until the big prop melted into a gray blur, the engine howled at full power, and the tail lifted high, floating in the air rush as asphalt began to stream beneath their wheels.

He eased the stick back, lifted it off, held the

P-51 at 100 feet or so, letting it run, gathering, savoring speed as landing gear and flaps whined up into streamlined position. As the farm fence flashed past under the wings, at well over 200 mph, he nudged back the control stick, let the plane climb, eagerly, heartily, soaring upward as though it could share his joy at the feel of it.

Surprising it came, serendipitous, he thought, to see the mist cloying so soon, so quickly after lift-off from the runway. Hastily, before it's fog could fully hide, he glanced across the wide, peaceful, blue of the river, eyes eagerly probing toward the City. It was not that It was truly shining, in any way alight or glowing. Unmistakable, though, even from the distance, was an engulfing sense of splendor, of radiance, of permanence, an impression of lovely dwellings, of tree lined streets, of lush greenery...even more, an aura of peace that radiated vigor and vitality and life, beginning rather than end.

What riveted his attention, though, as the last wispy vision of it faded into the mist enfolding the plane, was a thought long held, a thing he'd never have shared. The idea grated cross-grain to most envisions of The Place. But, to his way of thinking it had always seemed a bit much, even for There.

It's streets were lovely, solid, secure, peaceful to be sure...but they were not paved with gleaming gold.

CHAPTER FOURTEEN

OK, GOOD BUDDY." Was it the sound of a yawn that muffled, elongated the Angel's words? "We'll put 'er on automatic pilot again."

Thorsby watched the airspeed indicator settle down to the plane's 265 mph cruise speed, leaned back in the seat, relaxed as best he could, thinning gray-brown hair tilted against the rough, padded, khaki colored canvas of the headrest. The horrendous, raging, unbelievable rush of the encompassing mist seemed not so fearful now, less distracting, yet hardly a thing possible to ignore.

Yes! It must have been a yawn. Resonant, placid, rhythmic snoring echoed from the back seat.

Thorsby, himself, was far from sleepy, thoughts abounding with the wonders he'd shared in those few hours. He was glad to be, in a sense, alone...for time to reflect quietly, pondering. As he pondered it, he was gripped with eagerness to tell someone, everyone, to shout it to the world, or at the very least, to share such marvelous happenings with family, close friends, neighbors. It was, of course, a quite primitive impulse given the unbelievable events of the day.

As Thorsby and the P-51 and the Angel were propelled back toward that verity at something less than the speed of light, he wondered how many others, since the long-ago First Christmas, had seen and heard and shared such a bewildering celestial encounter.

CHAPTER FIFTEEN

GLIMPSES OF BLUE SKY drew his eyes overhead, up through the clear bubble of the plane's canopy. The gushing, ensnaring shroud was thinning again, perceptibly slowing, loosening, disjoining, becoming wispy, unraveled like a child's wicker Easter Basket drenched with rain. A tiny flickering on the instrument panel, the white needle of the airspeed dial, drew his gaze into the cockpit again. It had spun, not in a single leap, but in 5 or 6 seconds, from 265 to well over 450 miles per hour. Curious! The perceiving, the science of it, gnawed languidly into his awareness as the airspeed indicator surged quickly, resolutely higher. Just as quickly he was at full alert, feet pressed firmly to the rudder pedals, stick gripped tensely in his right hand, left cupping the black throttle bar.

There should, he judged, have been a slamming jolt, like tossing a child's toy plane out into a 200 mph hurricane. When the plane, with it's huge propellor, was spewed out of the hurtling mist into far slower, meandering, earthly air, it should have been like hitting a brick wall.

And yet, there was none, just the same gentle yaw and bounce and shudder he'd noticed coming out of the cloud at the other end, along the wide ocean-blue of the river. There must, he reasoned - if science and reasoning had any part in this strangeness - have been a flood of faster air thrust out with them, carrying, cradling, sheltering, blending prudently with slower moving air, easing them gently back into the worldly atmosphere he knew.

It was with a tingle of cheer that he recognized the sandy, parched, green-brown, uneven woodlands, ...tall, stately pines, smaller scrub-oaks, the tiny sun-glinted forest lakes of Northwest Florida. Far off, ahead and to his right, at two o'clock low, another lake glimmered in the afternoon sun. It is a much bigger lake, but the curious thing about it, the unexpected thing, is it's unique, near perfect, unlikely, roundness. He'd wondered often, over the many years he'd known it, if the green, watery depths clutched the secret of a meteor strike a million or so years before. Far more likely, though, the city-cloistered lake may well be the graceful remnant of an ancient Florida sinkhole, a caving of the limestone roof of a far underground cavern, the providential, symmetric, hour-glass sculpting of soil as it funnels deep into the bowels of earth, forming, perfectly rounding, the shoulders of a broad, sand-earth cup as it pours downward.

The singular persona of the lake told him where it was, where he was, and just as surely, the name of the wee city whose streets clustered upon it's sun-shimmered circumference.

The sight of it reminded him, and his mind played again the tale of the town resident who decided that life was not worth it all...whatever it was. In awful despondency the man had stepped into the waters of that utterly round lake from the boards of a city pier.

It was far too late when they found him. But there was an odd thing, a thing even more unexpected than the lake's roundness. In the silence after life has gone, in the cold of the waters...he was found still standing, shoes on the bottom, head upright three or four feet under the water's surface.

It was somber, a painful tale to be sure, but one which paralleled the passage of his own dark dismay in the days before, even in the early hours of that very morning. In the passing of a month or so of restless nights and apocryphal dawns he'd wondered, sometimes intently, whether that same course might be the answer to his own uncertainty. But then, that was before...the hours of this day!

He glanced at the altimeter. The white, hurrying veil had spewed them out into home air at 17,000 feet. As he calculated - guessed might be a better version of it - at the distances and direction of their flight, it seemed clear they'd come no closer than ten miles to DeFuniak Springs and it's round lake. They were east of it, flying at a southwesterly angle that surely, he thought, must rendevous again with the Bob Sikes Road and the abandoned little base twenty miles or so south of town. As the airspeed whistled downward past 375 mph he nudged the stick forward, a bit too eagerly, perhaps, to begin their descent.

In the grand way of fortune - or was it the touch of a mightier hand? - it was, without doubt, the random act which saved him.

CHAPTER SIXTEEN

THE UNFORESEEN, WRENCHING him out of his reverie, his torpor, was as sudden, shattering, as stunning as the violent, unimaginable explosion of the target truck just a few hours before.

At first, for a second or two, there was just the quiver of unexplained uneasiness, a queasy sensation of something unknown, looming. Like sensing another near being, unheard, unseen, in the pitch black of a moonless night. Like the anxious skittering of a chipmunk who feels, not yet seeing, the hawk diving silently, swiftly.

Mystified by the muffled, near murmured drone, a ruminating wail fused into it's barely audible timbre, his attention surged, eyes intent, quickly scanning instruments. Was the odd, expanding sound a menace in the machinery of his own engine? Oil pressure, temperature, RPM...everything in the green! A swift glimpse across the dials spent five precious seconds.

It was a new sound...sudden, rash,

reckless...a pulsing, staccato, metallic chatter behind him that jerked his head up, around. It was just in time to glimpse glowing darts of fire flashing in neat rows, side by side, just above the bubble of the canopy...erratic, stuttering dashes and dots, like a visible, airborne Morse Code. Puzzled, in the detached, surreal sense of a slow motion movie, he eyed yellow-red streaks of fire winking past close enough to whisk dust off the canopy...if any could remain in that rush of air.

The Sun was far into it's afternoon, light slanting softer, more yellow, now...yet still sultry, vibrant in the habit of Northwest Florida's near tropic late spring and summer and early fall.

Still gripped in the odd sense of slow motion, he watched the flickering rows tilt, easily visible even in the sunlight, the right rolling downward, left rising. The P-51 shuddered uneasily. Sparks erupted, blew back in the slip-stream. Out on the far tip of the right wing three small ragged holes streaked into the plane's aluminum skin.

At the same instant a presence, massive, shadow-like, looming, overpowering, swept upon them. Abruptly, he felt it's power, it's racing bulk, it's peril, behind, above his head....and with it an explosion of noise, the scream of an engine at full throttle, the continuing chatter that spewed out those menacing fingers of fire, the air-clatter of a great propellor, the rush and whine of metal slicing at high speed through the air.

The fancy to fly - at least in the deadly pirouette of aerial combat - must be attended by something more than mere fascination. There is a marvelous freedom about it, to be sure, the liberty to soar in three dimensions, high above the earth, far from the turtle-like restraints of land machines held fast in the clutch of gravity. It begs for steadiness, skill, a firm, knowing touch... boldness, driving determination, challenging audacity.

It was the last three he'd questioned, wondering sometimes - as many men have about themselves and war - whether he'd have the mettle for it.

On this day, instinct, resolve, tenacity, self preservation, leaped to his employ, unhesitating, immediate. His left hand drove the throttle bar full forward!...slipped instantly past it's round, black, rubber grip to flip up the small, red, metal cover of the gun arming switch. Just as quickly, as resolutely, his finger tapped it's small, cold, metal talon and the ruby-red gleam of it's warning glowed on the instrument panel, a certainty he could see out of the corner of his eye without glancing down. The big engine surged, it's grumbling purr rising swiftly to a full power howl. Another nudge of the control stick sent the plane into a steep dive, immediately the aggressor, pursuing, racing, instantly stalking the plane that had brushed so close, so recklessly.

"Hey! Hey! Hey!" Shocked from sleep by the abrupt rush of sound, the lurch of their own craft, alarm was unmistakable in the Angel's sudden shout. Thorsby could feel hands gripping the seat tensely behind his head, body arched forward, eyes peering with him through the windscreen. "What's goin' on...!" Clearly he was wide awake, now.

"German!" Thorsby's words hissed through clenched teeth as he banked the hurtling P-51 in a steep turn to the right tailing the fighter ahead as the two dove, now, as one.

"ME109!" the words hissed again, describing the most nimble, the most deadly German fighter plane of World War II. Invisibly linked by Thorsby's brazen, instinctive pursuit, like a long tail on a kite, the two diving planes passed 400 mph.

Thorsby rolled the plane sharply, banking hard to the left, centrifugal force of the turn a crushing weight, as he stalked the German. The glass of the ME-109's cockpit canopy glinted in the sun as the plane rolled and arched with serpentine elusiveness.

"That's it! That's it! Hang tight! Don't let him get behind us again...!" The Angel's voice was sharp, harsh in his ear, resonating with the need of it. "Attaboy! We're closing on him!" He could feel the Angel's aid...strong, tense, on the controls with him. "We're down to 12,000!"

The diving planes, giving up 5,000 feet of air in a few seconds, rolled hard again to the right, arching violently into the third twisting, zig zagging veer... just as abruptly back again to the left and upwards, brashly curving, hurtling up...up...up a steep cliff of sky, near hanging on props, engines screaming.

The German fighter slowed in it's sudden upward curve while Thorsby was still boring in at full throttle. He was far enough behind to sense the enemy's course, to tighten his own turn...to 'head him off at the pass'...in cowboy talk. The gap between them closed then...surprisingly, far faster than he expected.

Startled at the sudden nearness of the other, Thorsby palmed the stick back, pulled the nose of the P-51 higher, tighter in the climbing turn, tracking just to the left of the ME109's tail instead of directly behind.

Much closer, now, slowing rapidly in the steep climb, the warplanes surged upward, nearly abreast, like mismatched twins. At the top of their self-inflicted mountain of air, back at 17,000 feet, when the fighters wouldn't climb any more, nosing forward, leveling off, they were almost side by side, scarcely a wing length apart, all but hanging in the thin sky. The P-51 with Thorsby and the Angel was a scant 15 feet or so above, sliding almost imperceptibly sideways toward the other, drifted obliquely by the momentum of the climbing turn. They were so close, now, Thorsby could see a face behind the ME109's cockpit glass. He was far from an ace...but he knew enough about planes to know that it would be nearly impossible to recognize another pilot in combat behind the panes of a fighter cockpit.

In fact seldom, since sword's have been put away, does an enemy's countenance loom nigh, distinct, personal. Perhaps it is a saving grace...the palliative that makes dreadful, modern-day, weapons of war near palatable. To see the other's face, close-up, intimate, knowable, in the throes of kill-or-be-killed combat might be dismaying, unsettling for some, or maybe ruthlessly energizing for others.

Far more, an unseemly recognition of the

137

pallid, menacing face in the ME109's cockpit riveted Thorsby's attention. The knowing could not be from any personal connection. It was the black and white flicker of now-aged MovieTone news reels that leaped to his mind, the crisp uniform, the swastika, shrieking demagoguery, arm raised in self-hailing "Heil", a slash of inky black hair cornered down over the forehead, a narrow black square of moustache under the strong, prominent nose, fiery dark eyes blazing with an intensity that bordered on the maniacal.

"Hitler...?" Thorsby's voice rasped with surprise, eyes frozen on the squares of glass in the other's cockpit, on the face turned upward to him, on burning, hate-filled eyes that met, connected, gripped his own. The other plane's cockpit drifted closer, seemed to fill the space between the forward edge of the P-51's wing and it's long engine nacelle, just a few feet, too few feet, below. The odd thing was that his eyes seemed to magnify, to draw the face up, huge, close, almost as though outside it's cage of glass. It was as though Thorsby was meant to know who the German was.

"Hell, man...!" the Angel's shout rang in his ear, "Don't crash into him...!" Thorsby felt hands and feet on the controls with him again, but there was little to be done. The two planes floated up, slowly, inexorably over the crest of their mountain of air like two side-by-side roller coasters, speed near gone, barely easing over the highest hump of track, peering over the steep hill of the down side.

Thorsby's plane, still drifting sideways, passed over the German...it's glinting metal, it's slashing propeller, hidden directly underneath them for a long-drawn, uneasy breath. Thorsby, flinched, teeth clenched, waiting for the sound of clashing metal. None came. Finally, the glass panes of it's cockpit slid into in view again, below, to the left now, of the P-51.

"It is....it's Adolf Hitler...!" It didn't occur to Thorsby in the astonishment of the moment to wonder why that should be a surprise after the hours spent with Job and Plato and Columbus and General Billy Mitchell and Grandma Moses, ...his father and Suzie...near that wondrous Place. The pale, looming face had turned to glare up from the other side of the ME109's cockpit, dark malevolent eyes blazing.

"Yes..." the Angel was peering down with him, voice subdued, somber as the planes drifted farther apart, slowly nosing down, gaining speed once more, "...the Evil One has many faces."

The P-51's control stick and rudder pedals swiftly lost the slack, loose feeling of near-stall as air surged faster over wings, tail surfaces. Thorsby sat, a couple of seconds too long, transfixed by the face he'd seen. The German fighter's right wing lifted, up, high, higher. The plane rolled nimbly. Suddenly he was looking at it's belly, landing gear tucked deeply, flatly into the fuselage. The nose of the plane ducked, darted earthward...abruptly, the ME109 slanted into a steep dive. Until the P-51 entered the war, the ME109 could dive away from any plane.

"Tight! Hang tight...!" the Angel's voice was a shout again. Thorsby felt hands and feet override his own surprised sluggishness, thrust at the controls. "Stay with him...!" The P-51 snap-rolled onto it's back, nose arching instantly downward after the German. "We can't let him get behind us again...!" the Angel's tone was still tense as they dove steeply after the German.

"Could...can...can he shoot us down...?" The hint in the Angel's words was hardly a thing to be overlooked, in fact, would have given Thorsby quite a turn, if there'd been time for fear. He glanced up just a bit over his head as he muttered the question. Up was still an angle of down, at that point in the plunge, earth a mottled green-brown more than three miles away, straight down. The Me109's sudden maneuver had carried it the length of a couple of football fields ahead of them.

For a double brace of seconds the P-51's plunge had no - zero - feel of flying, far more like sitting on a brick, dropped from some towering skyscraper.

"Don't forget...," the words over his shoulder were curt, hurried, "with you in here the planes, the bullets ... they're hard. Going out. Coming in. His. Ours. Anyone can see us." The sound of the P-51's Rolls Royce Merlin rose quickly to a buzzing howl, the expanse of earth yawning rapidly wider in the windscreen, rushing up to them, the German in the center of it.

"Good Grief...!" an edge keened into Thorsby's voice, words snapped back over his own shoulder, "I'm the one who...!" He left it unsaid, palm nudging back on the control stick as the two planes dove through 10,000 feet at near 400 miles an hour, following the ME109 out of the dive into level flight...for a instant or two. After all, what words were needed? The Angel and Hitler, the two planes...good...or evil...were secure, beyond. Only Thorsby's earthly life hung in the balance, in the violent rush of those moments. "You said we'd get back in one piece...!" Even Thorsby felt surprise. It was more question than complaint.

"Well...," the Angel gripped Thorsby's shoulder as the two planes banked steeply into a sweeping right turn, then snapped back hard to the left in a wide curving arc, centrifugal force of the turns heavy, crushing. "We'll just have to win, won't we...?"

It was a subtle flicker of the German plane's elevators, a shadow of upward movement on tail surfaces, that gave Thorsby a fraction of a second's warning. Because of it, he hung tightly behind and the two planes surged upward as one, climbing steeply at full throttle. Fully unexpected, magically, suddenly, the ME109 was dead in the center of Thorsby's gunsight. His finger convulsed, clutching back impulsively on the trigger. 50 caliber machine guns chattered, making the P-51 shudder in tune with their rhythm. Blue smoke streamed back over shiny aluminum panels, rivets. Six fingers of fire leaped from the wing's leading edge, tracing outward toward the climbing ME109.

"No! Don't...!" Thorsby felt his finger jerked off the trigger by a force he couldn't see. The Angel's voice was a shout again."Not yet! We wasted too many on that old truck...!" The six fingers of fire, glowing tracer bullets, zipped past harmlessly, a hundred feet behind the German. "You ever hunt ducks? You gotta lead 'em, pal...aim ahead of 'em at these speeds."

Thorsby felt a tiny rush of regret, embarrassment, at an error the untrained could hardly be expected to know. He didn't say it. Truth was, there was no time even for an "oops." He followed the ME109 into a tight half-loop upward, snap rolling over, upright, at the top. The German zig-zagged sharply, steeply left, right ...then flipped upside down, half-looping into a dive again with the P-51 hot in pursuit, even a bit closer now. As the two hurtling planes drew level again, Thorsby's glance flicked to the instrument panel. Just 7,000 feet now, near 450 mph.

The ME109 rose suddenly, swiftly. "UhOh...!" The Angel's voice sounded clenched, like a fist. "He thinks he's worn us down! Gonna loop, up, over. Try to come down in back of us...!" The German surged upward, trails of white mist suddenly streaming from his wingtips, condensed by high speed, the skidding pressure of his arching rise. "Left! Break left...!" Thorsby could feel the Angel's strong guiding pressure on the rudder pedal, forward pressure on the control stick, easing an upward loop into a wide climbing turn. High speed made the arcs of both planes far reaching, longer than they might have been otherwise. "His eyes are right in the sun," the Angel chortled, "he won't see a thing until he's coming down out of the loop."

The German was high, upside down, nosing into the downward half of the loop, seeming to float, now, at half the speed. "He's gonna be surprised when we're not in his gun-sight or behind him either...!" the Angel chortled. The ME109 arched downward, rolled hard, deeply right, then just as quickly, harshly to the left. The two in the P-51 could sense, in their minds almost see, the German's head bobbing and twisting, eyes darting, searching frantically for them as they slid in behind him again. "He spotted us! There he goes...!" The German banked steeply to the right, racing away, even as the Angel's nudge on the control's sent the P-51 in blistering pursuit, scarcely 300 feet behind.

Moments, then, came frantically, cascading, tumbling one upon the other like gushes in a waterfall, fiercely lived, racing, violent, stressing to the edge of endurance. Thorsby could never, afterward, remember how many there were, seeming an hour of moments, surely less than five. The German zig-zagged hard left, right...like

a fast running hound trying to shake off a howling cat clawed onto his tail, dodging, feinting,
twisting into screaming turns, zooming upward,
to roll over, dive again...with the P-51 bonding
after like a caboose on the Sunset Limited. There
was no doubt, now, that it was the Angel's skill,
his over-riding pressure on the controls that kept
them clinging there.

"This guy is good...,"Thorsby muttered more
to himself than to the Angel, breathing fast, gusty,
laboring, muscles throughout his body hard,
clenched against the buffeting, the heavy weight
of centrifugal force in the turns. In the intense
concentration of those seconds no answer came.
Less than 500 feet above disaster, now, at 400
mph, trees and ground were a green-brown blur
streaming past. After all, the anxious thought
soared, the German sitting in the fast moving seat
just ahead was near an infallible military strate-
gist in the opening years of that War.

Another thought rushed in upon the doubt.
Battered by years of war, confused by the pres-
sures put upon him, hadn't Hitler made appalling, fatal, mistakes?

It was then Thorsby saw it. Wasn't there a
hint of fatigue, now, a discernable pattern, dodging, weaving? Roll, zig-zag right..., left..., right...,

then hard into a turn. Climbing, now, at a shallow angle. Roll, zig-zag left..., right..., left..., then hard into the opposite turn.

"Ok Pal...," Thorsby felt the Angel free the controls. The words came quiet, measured, sure, from the back seat. "You've got it figured out...!"

The question leaped to mind, but there was no time to ask the Angel how he knew. Thorsby tailed the ME109 hard in it's zig to the right, a zag to the left ...held fast, straight ahead, as it rolled to the right again.

He was waiting...set...already banking, turning, when the German soared out of the zig-zag into the tight, hard, left turn. He pulled the gray blur of the P-51's prop up a bit, tighter into the turn. Thorsby let the other plane slide down through his gunsight, a bit below, pacing, aiming ahead, giving the bullets time to cross the three or four hundred feet of air.

"Now...!" the Angel's voice was still steady, quiet. The loud, metallic chatter of six machine guns echoed in the cockpit, added to the howl of the engine, the rush of air around the canopy. As Thorsby pulled the trigger, he could feel the jolt, the rattling outbursts of six streams of shells, the tremor of the plane. Blue smoke blasted back in the slip-stream from gun ports in the wing's leading edge. The spaced flicker of tracer bullets, along with their flood of invisible companions, slashed out over the closing gap between the two rushing planes.

The odd sense of slow motion gripped him again, startling antithesis to their hurtling speed. Thorsby's finger froze on the trigger as he watched the spinning arc of the ME109's prop, seeming lazy now, edge toward, near, close, closer,...into...the hard, deadly rows of fiery, slashing steel. Like ramming a metal rod into a spinning saw, suddenly there were bright winking flashes among the propellor blades, a dark wand, snapping, flipping wildly out of that whirling, winking blur. Instantly, the German plane began to shudder violently, like a dog out of a bath, vibrating so savagely that it's form appeared fuzzy, even as the flashing hits continued to trace back along it's engine nacelle.

A rush of liquid black oozed back over riveted metal, blew into the slipstream, splattered, darkening the cockpit glass. Bits, shards, of the plane's aluminum skin frayed away into the wind, then larger access panels of the engine peeled away as the plane slowed suddenly, stunned, still nosing upward in the climbing turn. The P-51's machine guns stitched neat rows of holes back along the German plane's fuselage to it's end, blew parts off it's tail section.

The chattering guns went silent, empty, just as an yellow-orange flash, a billow of black smoke blew out the side of the ME109's engine nacelle...a goodly cluster of small, dark objects hurled out with the blast. The prop froze suddenly in it's spin, two blades remaining of it's three, as the tail slewed around and the nose of the plane sagged tiredly downward.

It seemed to pause the length of a long sigh before plunging like a stone, in a dizzying spiral, yellow-orange flames surging back from the engine, a twisting coil of thick, black smoke trailing behind.

At the sudden staggering of the other, Thorsby chopped the throttle of the big Rolls Royce Merlin, banked the P-51 steeply to the right, outside the arc of the stunned ME109, hard again to the left, to circle above, slowing, as the German plane dove, spinning, more than 3,000 feet toward the hardness of the earth.

As the doomed plane plunged wildly, faster, more steeply toward the ground, white mist gathered around, cloying close to it's flaming fuselage, lengthening along it's tortured metal, growing, expanding, hiding, finally enveloping, until the ME109 had vanished into it's fleece.

Nothing..., not a hint of the violence,... appeared out of it's woolly lower surfaces. It hung there for a few more seconds,... a white, puffy, innocent little cloud 800 feet or so above the forest. In a few breaths it faded to empty sky, leaving merely the twisted spiral of thick, inky black smoke 2,000 feet high to mourn it's passing.

CHAPTER SEVENTEEN

RELIEF, FATIGUE, A WITHERING sense of finality, swept over Thorsby as he slowly circled the spot, watching the rush of air from his wings and propeller distort, disperse the twisting, smoky trail, briefly lingering evidence of the German's passing. Both he and the Angel were silent for a languishing moment. Like small fish to a shark, they'd been the intended prey. In the fortune's of a small, far-too-personal conflict, with the Angel's consummate skill, and surely power and strength greater than their own, they'd blasted evil back to whatever it's own timelessness might be.

In the savagery of such conquest, Thorsby found strange hollowness, a sense of the wasteful, futile, regret of man's centuries old bent to rise against his own in such deadliness. Of course, though - the idea pressed even more strongly upon him - when others strike first, surviving is the order of the day. And, a darned acceptable order it is.

"YaaaHooooo...!" the Angel's shout rang out, echoed loud, long in the small cockpit. At the same instant the P-51 snapped smartly over on it's back. There was no question, now, that helping hands and feet were guiding Thorsby's on the controls. The gray blur of the big prop ducked into a steep dive. The plane half-spiraled quickly again to continue in the same direction as it leveled off just 500 feet above the forest. At 250 mph the trees below were again a rushing, tumbling blur.

"YaaaHooo...!" the Angel's howl came again as the wing of the P-51 lifted, rolled slowly this time, gracefully, rising upward as it arched over onto it's back.

It was, Thorsby instantly knew, felt it in his spine, the victory roll, the fighter pilot's signal to his home-base compatriots that another score has been made. As he glanced up over his head, through the clear, upside down, bubble of the cockpit canopy, he glimpsed the asphalt runway of Auxiliary Field #1 flash past.

"OK, pal. She's all yours..." Thorsby could feel his hands and feet free on the controls again. The plane's speed carried them three miles southeast of the little base.

"See that...?" the Angel pointed a couple of

151

more miles down the Mossyhead Highway to a dark blue pickup truck moving toward them. "No doubt they saw us in the dogfight."

Thorsby began a wide sweeping turn back toward the field, letting their speed drift slower.

"Sure as heck they've sent someone to check us out," the Angel seemed resigned to it. "Let's get this baby on the ground." There was a bit of urgency in his voice.

CHAPTER EIGHTEEN

"LEMME TRY A TACTICAL approach...?" It was the quick, graceful landing maneuver Thorsby had silently cheered when the Angel first landed. The runway of the Auxiliary Field #1 hurried closer now as Thorsby flew towards it from the side, maintaining the scant 500 feet above the earth.

"That'll get us on the ground quicker," the Angel was leaning forward peering over Thorsby's shoulder, sizing up their situation. "You're gonna cross the runway at about the right spot," he added. "What's your speed?"

"A little under 180..."

"You hit the nail on the head, pal," even after the strenuous fight the Angel's enthusiasm was still intense. "Let the good times roll..."

As the narrow width of the runway flashed past again, this time under the wings, Thorsby pulled the P-51 up into a steep climbing turn to the left, rising swiftly, veering tightly. After the weaving, climbing turns of the dogfight this one, if not a breeze, was certainly far more familiar than it might have been in the early hours of that day. He felt the Angel's tentative touch on the controls, though, gently fine-tuning the plane's path. At the top of the turn, banked steeply, not quite upside down, wheels and flaps coming down, Thorsby glanced up through the canopy, eyes darting, searching for the runway's end.

There! Far closer than in a long straight-in landing, inside the tree line already, over grass off the runway's end, defining the importance of the fighter pilot's tactical approach.

Lowering swiftly, now, long engine nacelle seeking, aiming for the runway, the familiar wheezing crackle of backfire as throttle is pulled back. Floating, sinking toward the long slash of hardness in the midst of forest green, waiting for it's end to rush up. Slowing too much. A little more power! Just right!

Blue smoke puffed, rushed past in the wind as wheels kissed asphalt, bounced, wobbled, rolled firmly aground.

"I've got it," there was still urgency in the Angel's voice. "I'll taxi us back while you get out of the gear."

The Angel had slowed the P-51 enough to

wheel around in the opposite direction as Thorsby passed the hat into the back seat, loosened parachute straps, unzipped the flight suit, while the cockpit canopy seemed to crank itself open. Penny loafers clanked onto aluminum panels under his feet. By the time the fast rolling plane had rounded the blind turn among trees he'd already writhed his way out of the olive drab one-piece flight suit and pushed it back over his shoulder. Wriggling his feet into both shoes at once as the plane drew to a stop at the old flight line, he lifted himself up by the windscreen frame, stepped onto the parachute, out onto the wing, into the buffets of air stirred by the big idling propeller.

"We made a darn good team today, didn't we?" pale green eyes searched Thorsby's. The Angel was already sitting in the pilot's seat again.

"Yeah!" A smile wreathed Thorsby's face. "We sure did!"

"We'll look for the chance to help Eglin," the Angel's voice was clear, even over the throb of the powerful engine, "...pay-back for the damage we did to that old truck." His eyes had a mischievous gleam. "You wanna come help...?"

"I wouldn't know how to find you," Thorsby spread his hands, a questioning stance.

"I'll find you, pal," The Angel's words came with a wink and a big grin.

"Right!" Thorsby touched the fingers of his right hand to his forehead in a casual salute.

CHAPTER NINETEEN

IT WAS HARDLY MORE THAN a dozen long steps to the edge of the aged, cracked tarmac. Thorsby kept his back turned to the plane to protect his eyes. Stinging bits of sand and dirt blasted around him, slashed into the air by the blast of the propeller as the plane spun around.

He had just stepped onto weedy grass, still facing away from the moving plane when the dark blue Air Force pickup truck bolted through the old gate several hundred yards away. It raced across the old paving, jounced roughly over unpaved sand, arched in a tight curve until it was facing back the way it came, skidded to a stop twenty feet or so from the edge of the tarmac.

It was a young man, perhaps 25 or 26 years old, who leaped out of the truck, leaving the door gaping wide. He was near average in height, solidly built, a bit bow-legged. The blue Air Police uniform was stretched tautly over a hint of beer belly. He was wildly waving a heavy, Army .45 caliber automatic pistol.

"Freeze...!" the young sergeant ducked into a crouching position, shrieking wildly at the top of his voice, leveling the barrel of the big gun at Thorsby's chest.

And Thorsby did just that, like a statue, hands partly lifted from his sides so the agitated young man could clearly see their emptiness. The hole in the end of the gun barrel looked as big as the open end of a garden hose.

"Halt...!" The sergeant spun around, aiming the pistol at the moving plane, venturing fiercely to yell louder than the twelve thundering cylinders in P-51's Rolls Royce Merlin engine.

"Stop! Halt! Right there...!" he screamed again as the plane continued to roll smoothly toward the sharp turn in the trees.

BOOM! The pistol bucked hard in the man's hand, it's shot echoing loudly.

Thorsby saw the hint of mist begin to gather around the plane.

"Come back here...!" the young Air Policeman's voice was shrill.

BOOM! The big gun barked again.

The mist seemed hurrying, clutching, enfolding the plane in broad fleecy arms.

BOOM! BOOM! The gun bucked hard again,

twice, aimed directly at the center of the shiny fuselage, below the plexiglas canopy.

The moving plane was getting hazy, now, indistinct, hard to make out clearly in the small, rapidly gathering fog.

BOOM! The fifth shot was at nothing but white fleece.

The sergeant stood frozen in his firing crouch, gun aimed, staring wide-eyed at the mist as it unfurled, blanched, became loose, wispy, lacy, faded, vaporizing. He stood, still crouched, stunned, as the last wisp dissolved, disappeared, leaving nothing but clear, warm air in it's place. There was nothing of shiny metal, no sound of it, just the unfettered view of trees, the broad, aged, concrete squares of the tarmac, weeds growing in cracks of its surface. Into the void came the song of birds. The Air Policeman's head bobbed, twisted, hurriedly, this way and that, eyes darting, searching frantically.

At last..., uncertainly, the young sergeant stood erect, hand holding the gun sagging tiredly to his side, face turning haltingly toward Thorsby, eyes wide with confusion, dread. He backed away a half dozen irresolute steps, eyeing Thorsby like a hiker might gape at a coiled rattlesnake.

"Sir...were...were you on that plane...?" The

question was deferential, now, eminently respectful, far from the bellowed demand of moments before. The gun was no longer aimed, rather waved, gestured toward where the plane had been.

Thorsby waited, a long breath, before answering the halting question.

"What plane...?" he shrugged, hands lifted wider in a divined gesture of mystification.

His step toward the young man was tentative, prudent, careful not to move quickly, to alarm, seeing the bewilderment, fear in his eyes. The Air Policeman backed two steps farther away.

"Have I done something wrong...?" Thorsby asked the question with a look of contrite trustfulness. "I was stationed here years ago. The gate was open. There's no sign saying I shouldn't come in...!"

The answer was long in coming, the man's eyes wide, round, near glazed. He fumbled three times to get the pistol back in it's holster. His stance said plainly that he thought it would be far better not to start anything..., even with a gun.

"You...you won't be here long...will you...?" the question was hurried, querulous, as he backed to the truck's open door, nearly leaping into the drivers seat.

"I was just leaving...!" By then, though, Thorsby was speaking toward a truck in reckless motion, spewing twin arcs of dirt and dust behind spinning rear wheels. Tires screeched as the pickup hit the old paved street, sped across the little base, out through the gate, leaving ponderous silence again in it's dusty wake.

CHAPTER TWENTY

THORSBY STOOD FOR A LONG moment, looking at the space the blue truck had filled, only movement the wrinkling of his nose at the pungent scent of the engine exhaust.

Satisfied, at last, that it would not return Thorsby paced with measured, pensive steps to the small blue car. The languor of weariness, onus of the extraordinary, the feverish, the astonishing, bore down heavily.

The ennui was momentary, though, fleeting, like catching one's breath at the end of a spirited 100 yard dash. It felt good to heft himself backward onto the trunk, brace heels on the bumper, revel in meager reality...feeling the car's springs give, ease a bit under the burden of his weight. After the ardor of those hours he felt suffused, slaked, full to running over, more so than one could measure without time to take it in, assimilate, sort out the factual, its deeper meaning.

The pleasant sense of loosening, of composure, of serenity settled upon him, bit-by-bit to be sure, like ice melting in tepid water.

In lingering, slackening, basking in the quiet, the scent of pine, it was not surprising that the contrast of suspicion, of doubt grew, festered.

Had this curious, bizarre day been real...? Or some irresolute dream, standing here in the sunshine, under wind rustled pine boughs, the mind in a far off place? He pondered it for a while.

But then, surely, hadn't long hours of the day gone, vanished, unaccounted for unless one could fully embrace the inconceivable?

Just as sure though, as absolute, was the sweat stain of stress upon his clothing. His hands responded in impulsive reflex to the thought, reached to feel the damp of his shirt..., under the arms, the collar, the pearly row of buttons, between the shoulders where he could reach.

In the inquisitive exploring of that certainty, the stain of sweat deep in clinging fabric, his hand patted a small firmness in the chest pocket of his shirt. Fingers reached in curiously, wondering.

It was not until the small, sky-blue card was out of pocket, before his eyes, that he remembered its fragility, nearly crushed under a shoe as he'd climbed into the curved aluminum of the P-51's bucket seat. Its likeness was all too familiar, known, an old, old ally.

He'd kept his own just like it for decades, moved lovingly from hiding place to treasure trove, from wrinkled envelope, to dresser drawer, to battered cigar box, year after year after year until it's sky-blue was faded, softened.

When had it vanished...lost in some itinerant move, some idle misplacing or house dusting..., along with it's little gathering of petty pocket treasures, meaningless to anyone else?

Thorsby peered at the card held between thumb and finger. "FLIGHT LINE PASS" it's larger letters decreed.

"Alabama Air National Guard," smaller letters whispered...but with pride and certainty that could not be ignored.

And then..., the place, "Eglin Auxiliary Field #1."

Following was the bold, sweeping, precisely penned signature, "1st Lt Robert M. "Rob" Addison."

"July,1949"

This card was not aged, faded, softened by it's years. Like the P-51, it was new....color bright, crisp, fresh-inked.

He wondered long at it's irrefutable reality, a

firm, palpable grasp between hope and promise, a tangible bridging of ethereally linked worlds, one far from consummate, finite...the other complete, infinite.

Thorsby, for the first time in many weeks, found himself eased, mellowed, at peace with the everyday we all know, even the astounding universal he'd barely touched.

At first he was quietly engulfed with the sense of excitement...framing in his mind who he would tell...just how he would break this wondrous news.

But then, as he sat cupping a raised knee in clasped hands, gently rocking atop the car's blue trunk...thinking... and thinking...and thinking about it...he knew.

Anyone, even his own wife and children, would be sure...far more than sure, he judged... that he had slipped over the edge of sanity if he tried to describe this day. After all...It is so easy to talk and sing of Angels on Sunday morning in the Good Lord's place of worship.

But in the light of day?...in a fighter plane?...right to the very banks of the Pearly Gates?...shooting down that Me 109 and its Hitler/ Satan pilot?.... Yeah right! Thorsby chuckled, thinking he could almost hear the door of the "funny farm" closing behind him.

Far more than likely...to speak of this day's miracles would brand him as a crank at best, a complete, absolute, wild-eyed nut at worst. He was sure now...they would look at him just as the sergeant with that big pistol had.

Faith, things Unworldly, he finally decided, were mostly clutched to human breast as an aberration, an odd conjunction of acceptance and doubt...a wavering joust of dream and hope.

Yes, indeed! The grasp of it was firmly settled in his mind. Sadly enough, this was a happening that - in self defense - would have to remain his alone.

The sun, just above the horizon, cast weak yellow rays through pine and scrub-oaks, tinting the high, fat, bulk of the water tower, stretching long, sunset shadows onto the small, long empty, air base. It hovered through tranquil, languorous minutes of earth's day when dawn and sunset are so much akin, bringing just a hint of cooler air so welcome to a man with sweat-damp shirt.

He glanced at his watch, smiled. On Fridays supper was usually an hour later, just time enough to get home. Keys to the small blue car jingled in his pocket as he stepped down from the trunk...reached for them.

It was not that Thorsby had any better grasp of what tomorrow might bring. It was just that he knew, somehow, some way..., it would work out just as it was meant to be.

And, as he started the engine, drove out through the time worn gate of the little base he wondered if the Angel would be allowed to keep his bargain to return.

About The Author

The author's third book, "An Angel with Silver Wings" is a first venture into fiction. Still, in it's pages, he continues to write about a region loved for more than five decades, Northwest Florida's magnificent Emerald Coast.

His first, "Villages By An Emerald Sea" remembers history of that delightful realm, much of it's glistening shore and emerald sea now vastly grown into America's elegant new Riviera.

The author's second, "Fun and Adventure in the Condo Lifestyle" is a compendium of "self help" and "how to" essays on effective condominium and homeowner association management. Even more it is crafted as a fun, interesting tour of condo life in America.

His fourth, "Wilson Shannon Baughman and...THE BOYS FROM LAKE COUNTY" will be a history of Company A, 73rd Indiana Volunteer Infantry Regiment in America's Civil War. It is scheduled for publication near year's end, 2004.

In fact, the author was born in Richmond, of an old Virginia family. Fourteen growing years were spent on a 60 acre family farm in it's rural suburb, Varina, a region resplendant with history. The Indian maiden, Pocohontas lived in Varina with her pioneer husband John Rolfe in the earliest years of our nation. It is also the community where Thomas Jefferson's daughter Martha lived with husband, Thomas Mann Randolph, Jr on his 950 acre plantation.

Many Civil War battles were fought in and near Varina, and the author's grandfather, James Wilson Baughman, built the main house inside a Civil War fort which remained on the farm.

After World War II, the author lived in Rome, Georgia, then Birmingham, Alabama. During four high school years he served in the Alabama educational system's Reserve Officer Training Corps and the Alabama Air National Guard.

In July of 1949, on a two week military sojourn, James Keir Baughman found Northwest Florida's magnificent Emerald Coast. In that same year his family bought acreage at Miramar Beach in South Walton County, just east of Fort Walton Beach.

On June 1st, 1951 his parents Elba A. and Iris Keir Armour Baughman invested in a small conglomerate of retail businesses in Shalimar, a suburb of Fort Walton Beach, and moved the family there.

The author began writing as an ad copywriter, columnist, news writer, and advertising manager at Fort Walton Beach's weekly Playground News in 1956. During an extensive career in business management, marketing, and advertising he published thousands of lines of copy as an advertising copywriter. In retirement he has written for national and regional magazines of the condo management and sailing genre.

He served 10 ½ years as a Fort Walton Beach

City Councilman, one year as Mayor Pro Tempore. Over the years, he served with many local civic organizations striving, as do so many of America's home town business leaders, to make the Emerald Coast a better place to live, work, and vacation.

His mother Iris Keir Armour Baughman guided the Greater Fort Walton Beach Chamber of Commerce for 14 years as Executive Director. He and his family members have owned ten business enterprises over the 52 year span.

The pinnacle of his business career, prior to retirement, was as a Florida Licensed Community Association Manager, managing two 7 story hi-rises in Destin. In earlier years he was a residential and rental condo owner and board member.

The author's love of sailing began five decades ago when he found Northwest Florida's now famous, emerald hued, waters. He and his wife Sandee live along side the Gulf Coast Intra-Coastal Waterway reaching 800 miles through five states to the Mexican border. Sandee's delightful mother, Mary M. Haitsch lives close by. Vitally active, driving her own car at 93, she shares much of their interests.

His children: James and wife Diane, Jill, Dana and husband Brent, are all Fort Walton Beach and Destin professionals or business owners who pursue his enchantment with the delightful Emerald Coast lifestyle. His granddaughter Mary Grace joined the family on March 30, 2003.

www.ingramcontent.com/pod-product-compliance
Lightning Source LLC
Chambersburg PA
CBHW020846260626
47169CB00003B/1154